Cree dashed for the epicenter of the flames.

The hairs on his forearms singed as the blaze closed in. Heat burned down his throat. It was getting harder to breathe, but he wouldn't stop. Not until he found her.

"Alma!" She was out here. She was alive. He had to believe that. He wasn't sure how much time had passed. He was going to find her. The fire raged as though feeding off the desperation boiling over inside him.

Coughing reached his ears from the left. "Cree?"

Every cell in his body homed in on his name. He'd heard her. It wasn't his mind playing tricks on him. "Tell me where you are!"

"Here." Another round of coughing broke through the howl of the inferno. Then he saw movement. A hand stretched toward him through the surface of the murky water.

"Alma." He hauled himself through the marsh and swam out to meet her. She was soaked head to foot, and Cree pulled her against his chest as the fire raged around them. "I've got you."

DEAD ON ARRIVAL

Nichole Severn

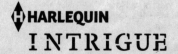

I dedicate this book to all the readers who let me kill them
in my books.

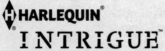

HARLEQUIN®
INTRIGUE™

ISBN-13: 978-1-335-58218-8

PLEASE RECYCLE

Recycling programs
for this product may
not exist in your area.

Nichole Severn writes explosive romantic suspense with strong heroines, heroes who dare challenge them and a hell of a lot of guns. She resides with her very supportive and patient husband, as well as her demon spawn, in Utah. When she's not writing, she's constantly injuring herself running, rock climbing, practicing yoga and snowboarding. She loves hearing from readers through her website, www.nicholesevern.com, and on Facebook, @nicholesevern.

Books by Nichole Severn

Harlequin Intrigue

Defenders of Battle Mountain

Grave Danger
Dead Giveaway
Dead on Arrival

A Marshal Law Novel

The Fugitive
The Witness
The Prosecutor
The Suspect

Blackhawk Security

Rules in Blackmail
Rules in Rescue
Rules in Deceit
Rules in Defiance
Caught in the Crossfire
The Line of Duty

Midnight Abduction
Profiling a Killer

Visit the Author Profile page at Harlequin.com.

CAST OF CHARACTERS

Alma Majors—She might be Battle Mountain's newest reserve officer, but discovering a body strapped with explosives at the bottom of a gulch throws her into a puzzle she never anticipated. And she can't solve it alone.

Cree Gregson—He lives with more than a few scars—mental and physical. But when his compelling, defensive next-door neighbor needs his help analyzing the bomb that nearly killed her, he's there.

Weston Ford—The only concern of Battle Mountain's police chief is keeping his town safe. No matter the cost.

Easton Ford—Weston's older brother will do whatever it takes to protect his fellow officers.

Battle Mountain—Rocky Mountain mining town comprised of 2,800 residents.

Chapter One

This was not why she'd joined the Battle Mountain Police Department.

Reserve Officer Alma Majors leveraged her heel into the dirt, trying not to fall flat on her face down into the gulch. She clutched her flashlight in one hand and tried to balance her weight with the other extended. Dirt collapsed under her, and the world tilted on its axis.

She couldn't hold back the scream lodged in her chest. Pain ricocheted around her skull as stars blurred into white lines over and over. She hit the bottom of the gulch. Air sawed through her chest. Her official first day on the job, and she'd already made a fool out of herself. Sounded about right. "Damn it."

Aches stabbed through her joints as she fought against the weight of her Kevlar vest to sit up. Dirt coated the inside of her mouth and dove deep into her lungs. Hand over her mouth, she coughed the worst of it up. Her flashlight had ended up a few feet from her. The beam cut through the darkness and cast shadows across rocks and boulders. Craning her neck over her shoulder, she gauged she'd fallen about fifty feet down a near straight incline. She rocked onto her sore hip and stretched for the flashlight.

What the hell was she doing out here? A year ago, she'd been happily married, with dozens of stamps in her passport, dirt under her fingernails and a career on the verge of surpassing the queen of Mexican archaeology herself. Alma brushed dirt from her uniform. Now what did she have? A one-bedroom apartment, a part-time job as the world's smallest town's rookie cop and no idea what she was doing with her life. "Well, at least I got the dirt part down."

The call about suspicious activity at the gulch had come in thirty minutes before, but from as far as she could see, there was nothing down here but broken bottles—evidence humans had yet to figure out where their garbage should be disposed—and what looked like a photo album that had been stabbed through with a kitchen knife. She shoved to her feet, stretching her neck to ease the pain.

Her radio crackled from her vest. "How you doing out there, Majors? Find anything?"

Weston Ford, Battle Mountain's police chief and her boss for the foreseeable future. The sleepy town of less than a thousand residents didn't have much in the way of a police department, but the work Chief Ford had done this past year had made national news.

He and his brother, the town's second reserve officer, had brought down not one but two serial killers in a span of months. When her world had ended, the former mining town had seemed like the safest place on earth. Until she'd decided to join the department.

Making her way around the boulders, she kicked into something ceramic and jarred the lid free. Dust burst from the container. She'd seen enough of them from her work as an archaeologist uncovering once-lost burial grounds within the Templo Mayor excavation site. Alma pinched the push-to-talk button between her thumb and index finger. "You mean apart from the urn I just found? Which looks to be full of someone's ashes."

The chief's laugh filtered through static and the call of crickets but didn't ease the knot of tension in her gut. "That would be Greta's husband. Last time I spoke with her at the diner, she told me they'd gotten into an argument, and she'd made him sleep outside. Kids must've picked him up. Thought it'd be fun to play hide-and-seek with her. Bring him back to the station if you can."

"Yes, sir." Was this what life was going to be like now? Nights filled with field trips into the bowels of Battle Mountain and something slimy stuck to her arm sleeve? As an archaeologist, she'd been an explorer, a truth finder. One of the best in her field. Only now, instead of uncovering ancient rituals, belongings and civilizations, she'd had to settle for—

she picked up something vaguely familiar—whatever this was. Nausea churned in her gut at the smell, and she tossed the raccoon's corpse as far away as she could. Nearing gagging, Alma wiped her hand down her pants. She doubled over to clear her lungs of decomposition. "That was really gross."

There was nothing out here. Whoever had called 911 about the suspicious activity must've imagined it. She'd make one more pass. After that, she'd head back to the station with Greta's husband. Alma ran her flashlight over the bottom of the gulch.

Only this time, something reflected back.

Twenty, maybe thirty, feet away, a metallic surface brightened under her beam. A small piece of jewelry? She'd seen all kinds of stuff she wouldn't have expected, but nothing valuable. Silence descended. Thick and unknown. Her instincts warned her to run in the opposite direction—the same instincts that had braced her for her ex-husband's violence—but the logical part of her brain said the 911 call hadn't been a hoax. Someone had seen something, and she intended to find the truth.

Alma forced one foot in front of the other, her flashlight steady on… A locket? The shiny silver chain had been buried in the dirt, but the main component had been left exposed to the elements. The petite oval shape clouded under her touch. A clear stone had been set in the middle. A diamond. Wedging her thumbnail into the grooves along the side, she pried it open. To find a photo of an infant boy inside. No more than a few months old, if she had to guess. "Who do you belong to?"

She caught the small manufacturer stamp on the back, the kind that charged upward of a thousand dollars for an item like this. No. This wasn't a gift picked up from the local big-box store. It was special to the owner. So what was it doing all the way down here?

A moan pierced through the night.

Alma automatically fisted the locket to grip her flashlight harder. Straightening, she tried to swallow a familiar tendril of fear charging through her. "Battle Mountain police. Is someone out here?"

No answer. No movement.

She pocketed the locket in hopes of returning it back to its rightful owner along with Greta's missing husband and unbuttoned the strap of her holster. The hairs on the back of her neck stood on end as she forced herself deeper into the gulch. Her pulse thudded hard behind her ears. "Hello?"

"Please," an unfamiliar voice said.

Alma locked onto an outstretched hand, fingernails clawed into the dirt. Every cell in her body protested as she followed the length of that hand farther up the woman's arm, to a section of red-crusted blond hair and then to hooded eyes. She collapsed beside the victim. Air crushed from her lungs as she reached for her radio. "Ma'am, my name is Officer Majors. Hang on. I'm calling for help."

She pinched the radio and opened the frequency. This wasn't an accident. This woman had been left at the bottom of the gulch to die. Why? "Chief Ford, I've got what looks like a 217. Assault with intent to murder. Please be advised, victim is conscious and speaking but in shock. I need an ambulance sent to my location. Now." Alma didn't dare move her, but the urge to comfort the woman had her setting one hand against the victim's shoulder. Blood seeped through Alma's fingers. "Ma'am, can you tell me your name?"

In a burst of desperation, the woman shot her hand out and latched strong fingers around Alma's arm. Hooded eyes widened as though she expected to see her attacker right in front of her. A lacerated lip split deeper as the woman pushed Alma back. "Run."

Alma landed on her rear, and the locket slipped from her pocket. The woman's gaze instantly homed in on the necklace, but where Alma had expected recognition, there was only peace. Acceptance even. "Ma'am, the ambulance is on its way. You're going to be okay. Tell me about the locket. Is it yours?" She leaned forward. "Is this your baby?"

The flashlight beam registered the small tick at the corner of the woman's mouth. Smile lines softened as she rested her head to the ground, her gaze unfocused. "Tell them I'm sorry… I wasn't strong enough."

The victim's final exhale hit her as though she'd taken a punch straight to the gut. Tears burned in Alma's eyes as she stared at the colorless face of a woman she'd never met. Alma sat straighter, her heels digging into the dirt as sirens echoed through the darkness. It was too late. She'd been too late. Her first day on the job, and she'd let someone die.

A series of beeps reached Alma's ears. She checked her watch, but she hadn't set an alarm apart from the one that got her up in the mornings. The beeping wasn't coming from her. She centered her attention on the hint of a light beneath the victim's shirt. It was coming from the victim. Alma rocketed forward. She skimmed her fingers over the woman's stomach and tugged her blouse from her jeans.

Red light haloed around her as she exposed the source, and she froze. "No. No, no, no, no."

Twenty. Nineteen. The timer on the clock ticked off second by second.

The tendril of fear she'd carried all night contorted into outright fear. Alma shoved to her feet, the locket still in hand, and pumped her legs as hard as she could. Boulders and small rocks threatened to block her escape, but she couldn't stop. Cold air burned down her throat, pressure building in her chest. She'd lost count of how many seconds had passed. Too few. The urn she'd nearly tripped over mere minutes ago stood stark against the uneven landscape, and she scooped it up as fast as she could. Slamming her hand over the lid, she tried to keep Greta's husband inside as she raced up the incline.

Her boots lost grip in the loose dirt. She cascaded back down a few feet, and a sob escaped without her permission. She hadn't survived her husband to die here. Not like this. Not tonight.

The explosion reverberated through the ground a split second before the blast knocked her forward. The urn slipped from her arms as she face-planted in the dirt. Heat and pain seared along her spine, and the world caught fire.

HIS ENTIRE APARTMENT SHOOK.

Cree Gregson shot upright in bed. The nightstand lamp hit the floor as he threw back the damp sheets. Single blast of an aftershock. Not an earthquake. Sirens punctured through the hard thud of his heartbeat behind his right ear. Shoving to his feet, he collected his jeans and boots from the end of the bed and dressed as fast as his grogginess allowed. Reality chased back nightmares of fire and pain bit by bit. "That was an explosion."

He was still in Battle Mountain, a small former mining town, with nothing more to lose. A thousand residents, limited resources and charm coming out of every brick down Main Street. Cree parted the bedroom sliding glass door curtains overlooking a small patio facing Henson Street. Thick trees, family-owned businesses and pristine mountain ranges attracted all kinds of people keen on hiding from the world. It was the perfect place to escape the past... as long as it hadn't followed him from Loveland.

A Battle Mountain PD patrol car raced in front of his building, emergency strobes flaring. Hell, it was close to midnight. Something had happened, and his gut said it had to do with whatever had shaken his house. Cree grabbed his keys from the top of his dresser in the corner and charged straight through the one-bedroom apartment and down the hall until he reached the front door. He slammed it behind him in a hurry.

"Cree, is that you? What's going on?" The elderly woman in the apartment across the outdoor corridor peeked her head through the crack in her door. Confident she hadn't mistaken him for an intruder, she stepped out into the halo of her lit, front-door sconce. The frayed edges of her floral nightgown swayed under the burst of a breeze as she clutched her equally old and equally well-fed Siamese. Stark white hair kept in rollers brightened under the addition of his apartment lights. "Was that an earthquake?"

"Go back to bed, Mrs. Faris. I'll check it out. Okay?" His gaze wandered to the apartment on the other side of his, but there didn't seem to be any sign of distress from the woman he'd run into a handful of times the past few weeks. Alma. He didn't know much about her. In fact, he knew less about her than he did about Mrs. Faris in the same amount of time, but there was an old compulsion he hadn't been able to ignore that urged him to learn the source of the storm in Alma's eyes.

A compulsion he wouldn't follow.

"You be careful. Don't be sticking your nose in something dangerous, you got me?" Mrs. Faris secured her door behind her.

In seconds, his knees protested his rapid descent down the stairs to the first floor and into the parking lot. He hit the unlock button on the key fob and hauled himself behind the wheel of the pickup that had become more than a way to get from point A to point B over the past few months. He threw day-old fast-food bags into the back seat as the engine growled to life under his touch.

He wasn't law enforcement anymore. While he was still technically considered one of Larimer County's bomb techs, he'd left that life and his need to get to the truth behind when his last assignment had blown up in his face. Literally. He had no jurisdiction and no business getting involved, but here he was ripping out of the parking lot and barreling toward the sirens.

Darkness encroached along the single-lane road leading to the east side of town. Grip tight on the steering wheel, he considered any number of possibilities for an aftershock like the one he'd felt. Gas explosion, a gasoline eruption after a fatal vehicle accident, a bombing. The police would have everything under control. So why was he still racing toward the other side of town?

The answer—no matter how many times he tried to drown it—knotted tight in his gut. Because it wasn't a gas explosion. It wasn't the aftermath of a fatal car crash. Every cell in his body had become all too familiar with that kind of physical discharge, even from a distance.

A bomb.

Town stores pierced his peripheral vision and failed to hide the massive rise of cliffs just outside of the city limits. From what he'd learned from the visitors' center, Battle Mountain had once been a rising star in the world of coal and energy, but when the mining companies had bled every last resource from the mines, it had become nothing more than a dying limb. Most of the police force had become resigned to finding work elsewhere. Town residents lost jobs, lost their retirement and their dreams. All in the span of months. The only thing left going for a place like this was acting as a pit stop to better pastures on the other side of Ten Mile Range. That, and the newly constructed veteran rehabilitation center out at Whispering Pines Ranch.

A firefighter stepped in front of his truck.

Cree slammed on the brakes. The pickup slid

along the curb before coming to a halt, and his heart shot into his throat. The emergency responder directed him to turn around, but he shoved the truck into Park instead. His boots hit the ground as he surveyed the controlled chaos of the scene. "Bloody hell."

Half a dozen fires burned along the edges of the gulch. A combination of firefighters and EMTs roamed through what was left of the debris littered across the desert landscape, but the focus seemed to be on one spot in particular. The point of the blast's origin? Instinct kicked him hard and had him stepping forward. "What happened here?"

"Sir, I'm going to need you to get back in your vehicle." The firefighter, dressed in full protective gear, motioned toward his truck. "This is an active crime scene and too dangerous for civilians."

"I'm not a civilian." He unpocketed his wallet and flashed the badge he'd tried to reject since turning his back on his former life, but there were just some things he couldn't escape. "Cree Gregson. Larimer County bomb squad."

"Of course. Sorry about that, Officer Gregson. We've already had residents start pushing the perimeter." The firefighter backed away. "You're looking for Chief Ford. He just arrived on scene. He's interviewing Officer Majors in the ambulance."

"No problem. I'll get the details from him. Thank you." Cree pocketed his wallet and headed for the single ambulance angled into the center of the street. Fire hoses roared over the orders and shouts coming from inside the gulch. From the look of it, the small canyon had been filled with all kinds of garbage even before whatever went off, but the perimeter of houses looked untouched other than a few shattered windows. Lucky break. In his experience, this could've been a lot worse.

The back door of the ambulance slammed shut, revealing a woman on the other side. Recognition flared, and Cree nearly missed his next step. Long, dark hair cascaded down her back, hiding a lean frame and Hispanic heritage he'd memorized the first time he'd set eyes on her. Bruises and scrapes interrupted smooth olive skin along the backs of her arms, right where the Battle Mountain PD uniform ended. His next-door neighbor was a cop. She hadn't stepped out of her apartment with curiosity after the blast because she'd been here. She swiped her brow with a white rag, coming away with blood, and Cree double-timed his approach. "Alma?"

Almond-shaped, brown eyes locked on his, then widened impossibly further. Full lips parted under a rushed exhale as she looked up at him. Tension visibly tightened along her dirt-smeared neck and shoulders. She twisted to scan the rest of the scene as she fidgeted with the bloody rag between both hands. "Cree, what are you doing here?"

"You two know each other?" A beige, ten-gallon

hat shadowed the police chief's face, but Cree had seen him around enough times to recognize Weston Ford. The man had reached legendary status in the short amount of time he'd taken over as chief, taking down two serial killers in the past few months to protect this town and its residents.

"Chief Ford, we haven't officially met. I'm Cree Gregson, Larimer County bomb squad." He extended his hand as he took position next to Alma. Visceral awareness had him memorizing the spread of injuries across her face and arms. Shallow lacerations and mostly dirt across her front torso and legs. She'd been front and center at the time of the blast, but her uniform and vest had obviously protected her against the brunt of the explosion. What the hell had she been doing here?

"A little out of your jurisdiction, aren't you, Gregson?" The chief shook his hand. "I've got Silverton sending me a team."

A humorless laugh escaped his control as he stepped back. "Yes, sir, and as I'm sure you'll learn when you call my CO, I haven't been active in about eight months, but the team you have coming from Silverton isn't here yet. I am. I'm happy to help anyway I can."

The weight of Alma's attention raised the hairs on the back of his neck, and he risked a glance in her direction. A mistake. His gut twisted hard as he followed the line of blood from her temple down the curve of her cheek, and he physically fought the urge to swipe it from her face. Seconds distorted into minutes, an hour, as the chaos around them dissipated. Until all that was left was that same storm he'd noted in her eyes the few times they'd met before.

A low jumble of words pierced through the ringing in his ears, and reality punched its way back into existence. The chief took a step into his vision. "Officer Majors has already given her statement. She responded to a disturbance call here at the bottom of the gulch where she found a woman strapped with the device. As of right now, we have no way of identifying who the victim was or what she was doing here. Do you think you'll be able to give us something to work with?"

Alma ducked her chin, effectively breaking the spell she'd cast with a single look, and the constriction in his chest eased. Her hair fell in a long waterfall over her shoulder, and he caught a glimpse of evidence still clinging to her uniform.

"I'll need to take a look at the scene before I can verify Officer Majors's statement. Until then, you said you have no way of identifying the victim." Cree closed the distance between him and Alma, drawing her attention upward. "You're wrong." Ducking into the ambulance door, he tugged a latex glove from the nearest box and snapped it into place.

"What are you doing?" She flinched as he reached for her, her hand cutting to her sidearm. Alarm filtered across her expression as she glanced at Chief Ford then back to him, and Cree hesitated.

"I'm sorry to be the one to tell you this, but you've got a bit of victim on you." He nodded at the blackened curve of calcium as he took a step back to give her the space she obviously needed. "Or rather, stuck in you. That's a piece of bone shard in your shoulder."

Chapter Two

She'd nearly drawn her weapon.

It had been an automatic reaction, the flinch, the bracing against a possible threat. She hadn't meant to reach for the gun holstered at her hip, but when Cree had broken into her personal space, she hadn't seen any other option in the moment. Chief Ford hadn't seemed to notice, but Cree had. She'd noted it in the way his gaze had lowered to her hand, how he'd increased his distance between them, and it was then she felt that bone-jarring pity that came with her truth.

Embarrassment heated Alma's neck and face as she pulled her hair up and out of the way. The physical awareness of her next-door neighbor refused to let up. Even in the middle of a crime scene, she'd noted the perfect symmetry of his facial features, the exact shade of forest green in his eyes, how he double-tied his bootlaces. Of course, she'd trained to take note of minor details, but this…this was something else. "You never mentioned you were law enforcement."

"To be fair, neither did you." Cree folded his arms across his chest, his weight leveraged against the back of the ambulance door. "How long have you been on the force?"

Alma rolled her lips between her teeth and bit down. "Tonight was my first shift."

"Hell of a way to get on-the-job experience." He straightened to his full height, somewhere around six-two, maybe six-three. Valleys and peaks of muscle flexed and receded under his every direction, and a slow burn of appreciation carved through her. "I'm glad you're okay."

Sincerity drove through her defenses and tried to pry up the armor she'd girded over the past few years, but she'd been deceived by all the right people before. She wasn't going to give anyone else the chance to get under her skin. "You said you're with the bomb squad. Shouldn't you be down there looking for pieces of the device instead of making sure this guy uses the right kind of suture for my stitches?"

"It'll take days to collect all the bits and pieces," he said. "I'd rather hear your account firsthand."

"Okay, Officer Majors. This might sting." The EMT who'd seen to her minor cuts and bruises positioned one hand against her shoulder blade and extracted the bone shard with the other. "Got it." He preserved the bone shard inside an evidence bag and handed it to her. "We'll get you cleaned up once CSU has had a chance to collect any other evidence from your clothes and hair."

"Thank you." She focused on the rounds Chief Ford made through the scene as a shot of pain arced through her shoulder, but Alma held her expression. She'd been through worse. She'd survived worse. Although she hadn't been required to thread one arm out of her top and expose her sports bra for the entire town to see while she was stitched up in the middle of what looked like a war zone. That would normally happen behind the emergency room curtain, but she had to admit the urge to hide had faded over the past few minutes. She wasn't sure why. As much as she hated to face it, Cree was involved now. "All right, Officer Gregson. What do you want to know?"

"Cree." He centered himself in front of her. The fluorescent lights from inside the ambulance accentuated the ridges between his eyebrows and the deep recesses of his biceps. In another life, he might've been handsome. Now he just looked weathered. "Tell me what you remember about the device."

"Not much. I only got a look at it for a few seconds before I ran as fast as I could." In the few times they'd met in the corridor outside of their apartments, she'd kept the upper hand. Given as little information as possible while mining for details about the people around her. Couldn't be too careful. Mrs. Faris, for example, kept to a very strict routine Monday through Friday that consisted of walking her overweight Siamese on a leash each morning, followed up by locking herself out of her apartment directly after. Within the first week of moving in, Alma had resigned to making a duplicate key and hiding it underneath the loose knocker of the elderly woman's front door.

As for Cree… Well, she'd found herself learning a lot more about him than anyone else when she wasn't required to put in face time at Whispering Pines Ranch. How he took his coffee—black, one cream, one sugar at the diner—how he tended to wear the same pair of jeans with the stain on the right shin most of the week, and how much time he dedicated to his physical fitness at six every morning. No television, from what she'd been able to hear through their thin shared wall. Which left her wondering what a man like him did in his spare time. And why he'd come to Battle Mountain in the first place.

"Anything that stood out?" he asked.

She closed her eyes to cut her curiosity about him short. She hadn't left one relationship to immediately fall into another, and she sure as hell wasn't about to forget why she'd asked Easton Ford to train her to become a reserve officer for this town. "It had a rolling countdown. It looked like some kind of computer motherboard with an LED screen attached. There were coiling wires leading from it to a brick of white clay." She opened her eyes, steeling herself against his study. "It was set to detonate a couple minutes after I got there. It looked as though the device had been sutured into her midsection. The woman... She was almost dead, left there like garbage."

"You're lucky to be alive," Cree said.

She tightened her grip around the small shard of bone safely housed in the evidence bag. The crime scene unit would ask her for her clothing as soon as they were finished with the main scene, but for the time being, she wasn't going anywhere. The victim. Air crushed from her lungs, and the images she'd tried to block out flooded back. An earthquake of emotion pounded through her, one aftershock after the other. Tremors rocked through her until the pressure behind her sternum reached its peak. The shock of what had happened had already started wearing thin. "She told me to run."

"Hey." Cree crouched in front of her, so close. Too close, but at the same time not nearly close enough to keep her from shattering right here in the middle of the scene. He clamped his hands on either side of the rig's bumper, careful not to touch her. "Alma, I need you to look at me. Take a deep breath through your nose and let it out through your mouth." He notched his chin higher to level his gaze with hers, and the world stopped trying to tilt on its axis. For now. "This is not your fault. You know that. Chief Ford knows that. You responded to a call, and there was nothing you could've done differently. You understand me?"

She tried to follow his command, but her lungs wouldn't fill. Darkness filtered into the edges of her vision. What kind of police officer was she? She should be better than this, stronger than this. Sweat built along her hairline, her skin clammy. "She was still alive. I could've—"

"No. Because if you'd tried to get her out of there, you would've been caught in that explosion, too." His words failed to unwind the knot of guilt tightening in her stomach, but his voice kept her grounded. Gave her something to focus on other than the aimlessness inside. "Your brain is processing a trauma. I know this is hard, but all of the pieces will come back to you. Is there anything else you remember that didn't end up in your statement?"

She pressed her fingers into the ambulance bumper, one after the other in a repeating pattern. An old habit she'd used in the minutes before her ex-husband had stepped through the door each night. Her hand drifted to her cargo pant pocket, and she drove it inside. The thin chain threatened to snap under her grip, but she'd never let anything happen to the keepsake she'd picked up beside the victim. "I found this a few feet from her body. It's what drew my attention to her." She tugged the item free and offered it to him.

Cree met her halfway, and she dropped the necklace into his palm. Confusion warped his handsome expression. "A locket?"

."I think it's hers." The image inside had burned itself into the recesses of her mind, and an urgency she couldn't describe took hold. One she hadn't felt in a long time. "If the shard of bone isn't enough to identify the victim, do you think this will help?"

He coiled the necklace into his palm, holding it between them as he stood. "That depends. You can turn it over to the forensics lab to see if there are any viable prints other than yours or epithelial cells between the chain links, but it's a long shot. Until then your best bet is the bone shard and checking missing person reports."

Her best bet. Not theirs.

"Battle Mountain doesn't have a forensics lab. It'll have to go to Unified Forensics in Denver, which will take at least a week to run DNA." She took back the locket, the pad of her middle finger trailing along the main crease in his palm, and her heart jerked in her chest. "You offered your help to the chief back there until the Silverton team arrives. I'm guessing that expertise will be limited to the device once techs collect all the pieces."

The low vibration of heavy tires on asphalt combined with the slam of truck doors pulled his attention down the road. Two officers hauled equipment from the back of their vehicle, both sporting BOMB SQUAD windbreakers. "Actually, it looks like that's my cue. Like he said, I'm out of my jurisdiction. I'll fill the Silverton team in on the device you described and potential starting points of component suppliers. Otherwise, I'm done here."

"Right." Alma shoved to her feet, offering her hand. Raw nerves protested the action, but if she was going to move on with her life—to get back to being the person she used to be—she had to push herself out of her comfort zone. "Well, it was nice to officially meet you, Officer—" She caught herself. "Cree. I'm sure I'll see you around the apartment complex once this investigation is concluded."

"Probably sooner if Mrs. Faris locks herself out again." Cree shook her hand, callouses catching against the skin of her torn-up palms, and the sensation wasn't…unpleasant. He pointed behind her with his free hand. "I do have one more question for you, though. Is that an urn behind you?"

IN THE WORLD of 24/7, when the sun started breaking over the horizon, Greta's on Main seemed to be the only place in town to get a decent meal.

Black-and-white tiled flooring expanded the length of the entire diner, the red pleather seats and barstools reminiscent of the old days. Ancient recruitment posters from the mining companies peeled right along with oil-spattered paint above a border of matching floor tile. In a town like Battle Mountain, it was easy to get caught up in routine. Hell, Cree bet most of the customers already taking their seats at the crack of dawn had been showing up on the regular. It wasn't a matter of what they were going to do with their days. It was more like what were they going to order at the diner.

Cree slid onto the end barstool and pointed to the steaming pot of fresh coffee behind the counter as Greta Coburn herself closed the distance between them. He flipped the upside coffee mug in front of him straight up. "Coffee, please. Black with cream. Oh, and I've got something for you." He hauled the urn he'd taken off Alma's hands onto the Formica surface. "Officer Majors found your husband at the bottom of the gulch."

"Serves him right having to spend last night outside." Waist-length gray hair practically floated around Greta's thin shoulders as she tucked a notebook and pen into her apron and hauled the urn against her hip. "I told him what would happen if he watched our show without me, but the man never listens." Carefully manicured pink fingernails highlighted weathered hazelnut skin and offset the grunginess of the diner she'd dedicated her life to running since 1961. She set her husband's remains near the cash register, then shuffled toward the coffeepot and filled his mug. "What can I get you, boy?"

He studied the single-page, laminated menu that had seen better days. "What's good?"

"Go for the chipped beef," a familiar voice said from behind. "It's a town favorite." Alma stepped into his peripheral vision as she took the barstool beside him. The patches of blood he'd noted at the scene had been washed clean, and it looked as though she'd gotten the chance to change into something not covered in dirt and explosive residue. "I'll have the same, Greta. Coffee, too. Thank you."

Greta filled her mug, then mumbled her way back into the kitchen.

Cree stared straight ahead as he took his first sip of coffee. He should've known the risk of getting involved in a local case, but he couldn't deny the relief forging through him at seeing her stand on her own two feet. "Didn't expect you here." Whatever had happened in that gulch could've ended with two bodies instead of the one. He settled his coffee on the counter. "I already know what you're going to say. You can save your breath."

"You're giving yourself too much credit." Alma shifted herself on the barstool, resurrecting a hint of fresh soap and some kind of floral shampoo. Her hair was curlier than he remembered from the scene. Still drying from the look of it. The waves softened her features, but there wasn't anything that could take away from her overall beauty, even the nasty gash across her temple. She took a sip from her own mug and sighed distinct pleasure. "I'm just here for the chipped beef, like most of the people in this town. It's actually the only edible item on the menu. I think Greta stopped caring if people liked her food a long time ago, but it's the one thing her husband would eat at the end."

"You're a regular," he said.

"Born and raised. My parents brought me here every morning before school, all the way up through college. I can't tell you how many cups of Greta's coffee got me through my graduate program. Even after they decided to retire in warmer climates a couple years ago, I can't seem to stop myself. And after my divorce, I couldn't see myself leaving. Greta's has a way of working under your skin like that. Becomes who you are, just like this town." She nodded toward Greta and cleared a spot for her plate as the old diner owner settled what looked like a half-hearted attempt at biscuits and gravy in front of them. "Thanks, Greta."

"Whatever." Greta shuffled onto another customer.

"If I'm being honest, I think she and I are on our way to being best friends." He tried to pick out a single identifiable ingredient as he studied the mess across his plate. "What the hell am I looking at?"

Alma's laugh pierced through the confusion closing in and drove up under his rib cage. "Squares of top sirloin over white toast and mixed with gravy. It's a mixture of hot oil, flour and milk. The meat has a spicy kick that overwhelms the blandness of the gravy, but most people add salt and pepper for some taste. Go on. I promise you won't regret it."

"I'm going to trust you on that." He unwrapped his silverware from the napkin to his right and sliced through a thick slab of meat. Spearing a bite, he grated the tines of his fork between his teeth. Hell, she was right. The kick of the meat, combined with the flavorless gravy, combined to make one hell of a heavy and rich breakfast. "The toast isn't bad."

Her smile nearly shocked the life out of him as she took a bite from her plate. They ate in silence for a few minutes, switching off between spicy meat slop and coffee.

"You're divorced." He hadn't expected that, but he'd seen plenty of his colleagues' marriages crumble to ashes because of the pressures of the job. Late nights. Early mornings. Obsession with certain cases. Then again, Alma had told him last night had been her first shift. "I'm sorry to hear that."

Her shoulders stiffened, and she pressed the back of her hand against her mouth to stop the humorless laugh. In vain. "You're assuming he was the one who ended it." She kept her gaze on her own breakfast for a series of breaths, and Cree could practically feel the camaraderie they'd built at the scene icing between them.

He shook his head and sat back away from his near-empty plate. His chest tightened. Wiping his mouth with the napkin, he crumpled it in his hand as guilt raged. She'd reached for her weapon when he'd pointed out the bone shard stuck in the back of her shoulder. She'd tried to back away. At the time, he'd justified her actions because most people—trained or not—tended to suffer some kind of trauma after an explosion like that. But what if it had been something more? What if it had been a learned reflex? "I'm sorry. I didn't meant to pry. It's none of my business, and I shouldn't have asked."

"It's not something I like to talk about." Long fingers coiled round her fork, and Alma seemed to focus all of her attention on taking her next bite.

"Right. Then it's probably a good idea if I remove my foot from my mouth elsewhere." He raised his hand to signal Greta for the check and pulled his wallet from his jeans.

"The Silverton bomb squad is still processing the scene. So far they've got enough pieces to start reconstructing the device that had been strapped to that woman." Her voice deadpanned. "Seems they're more interested in putting it back together than finding out who the victim was it killed."

"You're right. I can tell you from experience, they are. As soon as they can trace the components, they'll have a better idea of who built it." He tossed a few bills onto the counter and stood. "You said last night was your first shift, which means you haven't worked a homicide investigation before. The only way you're going to be able to identify the woman at the bottom of that gulch is working backward."

"You're saying if the bomb squad identifies where

the device's components came from, they can determine who built it, then who would've wanted the victim dead," she said. "But what about the victim's family? What if it takes days, if not weeks, for the bomb squad to reassemble the device, to track each component and determine who designed it? Do they just get to suffer not knowing what happened to their mother or wife or sister?"

Frustration bled from her every pore, and Cree gripped the edge of the counter. That same desperation to do the right thing had controlled him. Right up until the clock on his last bomb defusal hit zero. An all-too-familiar flash of pain burned down his legs and across his chest, and he took his seat. Alma hadn't come to the diner out of some routine she couldn't shake. She'd come for a lead. "You've already been through the missing person reports."

Had she even taken a break since he'd left her at the scene? He'd been so caught up in the larger details of her features he hadn't noticed the traces of exhaustion in her eyes and the sluggishness in her body language.

"No one fitting her description has been reported missing in the past two months." She ducked her head, her food forgotten. "I tried pulling prints from the locket I found, but you were right. There were no usable markers to go off, and the bone shard the EMT pulled out of me will take weeks to process at the lab. Right now, I have nothing but a photo, and who knows how old it is. There's a baby out there with a missing mother, and there's nothing I can do about it until the bomb squad or the lab uncover a lead." She craned her gaze to meet his. "You have more experience with cases like this, Cree. I know this investigation is out of your jurisdiction, but I need your help. Please. Just tell me where to go from here, and I promise I won't drag you deeper than I already have."

Understanding seized his next breath. He hadn't come to Battle Mountain to get involved in a case. In fact, he'd run from Larimer County because of how his last one had ended, but his gut told him whoever had strapped that device to the victim had done so to destroy evidence of her identity. They didn't want her found, and the more Alma pushed to solve that mystery, the more danger the rookie would find herself. He leaned back on the barstool. Acceptance wedged itself in his joints despite his stern promise not to get involved with the people of this town for their own benefit. Then again, Alma wasn't just people. She was a puzzle all on her own his training urged him to solve. "Pay for your food. We're going on a field trip."

Chapter Three

Galaxy Electronics wasn't anything out of the ordinary. The narrow aisles and dusty shelves had been a reliable escape for her once upon a time. Before life had gotten so messy. Alma swung open the heavy glass door leading inside and immediately sucked in a thin veil of dry rot and dust. The bell over the door announced their arrival. "You think whoever made the bomb might've gotten the components here?"

"It's not much to go on, but most locals shop local, even when premeditating to commit a crime." Cree kept close on her heels as she scanned the disorganized masses of cables, wiring and computer parts. "Galaxy is the only electronics store in town. It's as good a place to start as any."

Her boots skidded against built-up debris across the cement floor, and Alma was nearly taken back to the long hours she'd spent in this very store reassembling a cuckoo clock for Mr. Thorp's wife. She'd always been good with her hands, and the store's owner hadn't a clue how to put the poor thing back together. As far as she'd been able to tell from research, the clock had been an original. Older than her. It was in the shadows of these dusty shelves that she'd found her penchant for the past, for digging through history, and trying to make sense of it in the modern world. "Most of the computer motherboards are in this aisle here."

The soft sound of footsteps filtered through the space, and a smile tugged at her mouth as she recognized her former employer. "Mr. Thorp. You probably don't remember me, but—"

"Dr. Alma Ortega, of course I remember you." Thin, papery skin enveloped both of her hands as he clasped her gently. The curve through his spine had gotten the best of him over the years, evidenced by how much…shorter he seemed to be than she remembered. The receding hairline she'd noted all those years ago was gone now with little evidence the seventy-year-old electrical engineer still had the ability to grow anything but white tuffs. "That damn clock is still waking me up every hour, but my wife wouldn't have it any other way."

"I'm so glad I could help her hold on to her wedding gift a bit longer," she said. "I know how much it meant to her."

His weak smile shook under his notice of the firearm at her hip and the badge clipped on the other side of her belt. "You're a police officer now?" His disbelief combined with the acid in her stomach, and she swallowed the grief charging up her throat. "What happened to archaeology like you dreamed?"

"That's a story for another day." She angled her upper body to face Cree, all too aware of him behind her. She tugged a crude drawing of the device she'd seen before detonation and unfolded the paper. "Mr. Thorp, this is a friend of mine. Cree Gregson. We're here because there was a bomb that exploded in the gulch on the east side of town last night. Unfortunately, there was a woman who was caught in the blast. I got a look at the device before it went off, and I'm hoping you might be able to remember if anyone was in here recently to buy some of the components."

She handed him the drawing.

Shock parted the old man's thin mouth and jarred the thick protrusion of skin underneath his chin. Age spots darkened in sharp contrast to Mr. Thorp's brilliant blue eyes, not just in color but in lividity. He fumbled for his glasses by sweeping his hand down the front of his button-down shirt pocket, then raised them to what was left of his hair. Centering the frames over his nose, the proprietor took the paper she offered and gave it a once-over. His balance waned as he backed toward a stool positioned under his old workbench nearby. "Your drawing skills have obviously transferred with your career change. This here looks like a run-of-the-mill circuit board. You can find them anywhere. Heck, you can find two hundred in this store alone. They're everywhere. Laptops, medical devices, home appliances and such. Even those touch-screen things people are carrying around now days. I've been recycling people's old stuff for years now and breaking them up for parts. What makes you think whoever built this bought it here?"

"Yours is the only electronics store in Battle Mountain." Cree maneuvered to her side, his bare arm brushing against hers. "In my experience, bomb builders shop local. Someplace they're familiar with and know they can get what they need."

Mr. Thorp shook his head as he hauled himself off the stool. An exasperated groan followed suit. "I can pull receipts for the past couple of months, but I'm not sure it'd help. I may be getting old, but I remember every part and cable I sell. No one has purchased this size circuit board for a while."

"Is there anyone else who works here with you?" Alma offered her hand for balance as Mr. Thorp trudged to the back of the shop. "Someone you might've hired to help with the long hours or inventory?"

"Not since you up and left for graduate school, young lady." A low laugh accompanied Mr. Thorp's shuffle to the outdated Sanyo ECR-240 cash register he'd kept from the eighties. "No one in this town is interested in learning the way things work anymore. They're too impatient. When something breaks, they just buy new and move on with their lives. Don't even bother trying to figure it out themselves." He pulled a beaten shoebox that she knew still contained receipts from under the counter and offered it to her, the drawing still in hand. "You were something, kid. If you hadn't gone off to school, you'd be running this place yourself, and I'd be on a beach, as far as I could get from the damn cuckoo clock."

Alma couldn't hide her smile. The sincerity behind his words brought out a nostalgia she hadn't let herself think about in a long time. The staleness in the air worked deep under her skin and into her lungs, calling on better days. Happier days. She'd been a teenager when she'd worked here. She'd taken apart and reassembled almost every device she could get her hands on, but after a while, even she had needed to escape the small-town suffocation. The whole world had been waiting for her, and she'd taken it. For a while. In the end, though, she'd known she'd end up right back here. Where it was safe, familiar. She hefted the box higher. "Do you mind if we borrow these for a couple of days as well as any security footage you might have?"

"No problem. The tapes are in the back. You can grab them before you go." A gruffness that hadn't been in Mr. Thorp's voice registered as he used the counter for balance. "As for the receipts, I don't have to do my taxes until the end of the year. Then it's my accountant's problem." He pointed at Cree with the drawing. "You said you had experience with this kind of thing. What is it you do?"

Cree straightened a bit taller, his eyes cutting to the dust-bunny-coated floor. He shifted his weight between both feet and set a coil of red wire back on its shelf. The same kind of wire she'd drawn from memory in that sketch? "Bomb squad. Larimer County for the past decade. Explosive Ordnance Disposal before that."

"Ah, army man. I thought so." Mr. Thorp notched his chin higher, crossing his varicose-veined arms over a broad chest. "Where abouts?"

"Camp Bondsteel. Kosovo." Cree leveled dark green eyes on her, as though he hadn't meant for that detail to slip, but there really was nothing he could hide from Mr. Thorp. The old man had the eyes of an eagle and the nose of a bloodhound when he caught on to something that interested him. It was one of the things that had made him such a great electrical engineer. The patience. "The 720th."

"Ah, cleaning up the mess left behind, were you? Hard work." Mr. Thorp nodded. "But I guess those mines weren't going to take care of themselves."

"You served?" Interest flickered in Cree's eyes, and for the briefest of moments, Alma swore that same interest had centered on her while the EMT had been removing a shard of a person from her shoulder.

"Vietnam." Mr. Thorp unbuttoned the sleeve of

his shirt to show off the intricate but faded tattoo underneath. "20th Engineer Brigade."

Cree saluted, standing at full attention, and the warmth in her chest spread. "Thank you for your service, sir, and for your help with the device. If you don't mind, I'll grab those security tapes from the back."

"Straight back, son. Can't miss 'em." The ancient store owner pushed himself to his feet and slowly closed the distance between him and Alma. He offered her the drawing back as Cree disappeared into the employees-only section of the small shop. "I like him."

"He's something else, for sure. We'll have your receipts back to you in no time." She set her free hand over Mr. Thorp's wrist. "If your accountant gives you any trouble, send him my way."

He handed off the drawing. "I'll keep an eye out for any of these other components. You said you got a look at the device. You were there when it went off?"

"Yes." She swallowed remembered panic before the countdown had hit zero and pulled her shoulders back. "But I'm fine. I made out. Not everyone who was there can say the same."

"This work you do now… Are you sure about this? Because I wasn't kidding before. I die, this place is yours. You're the only one I trust to know what to do with all this crap." His smile wavered with effort and then was quickly replaced with concern.

"You worked so hard to accomplish your dreams. Maliya and I never had children. You and this place were all we had. We are both so proud of you. We just want to know you're happy."

Alma forced a smile as her eyes threatened to burn with tears. The weight of her weapon demanded attention from her hip, a heavy reminder of why she'd left her life behind. "This is for the best."

Heavy footfalls penetrated the bubble she and Mr. Thorp had built apart from reality, and Alma zeroed in on Cree racing to the front of the store.

"We need to leave. Now!" He threaded his hand between her rib cage and arm and thrust her toward the entrance. Cree ducked in front of Mr. Thorp and hauled the old man over his shoulder. "Go!"

"What's going on?" She shoved through the dirt-caked glass door and out onto Main Street, Cree close on her heels. The muscles down the backs of her thighs burned as he raced ahead of her into the street and set Mr. Thorp behind a parked vehicle on the other side. She followed suit, protecting her former employer with her body as much as she could.

Cree raced around the street side of the car and swung his arms wide as he directed residents away from the building. "Get back! Get out of here! It's going to—"

Fire and heat exploded outward in a cloud of black smoke and deafening rage.

In an instant, Galaxy Electronics was gone.

THE SCARS ALONG his back burned in memory.

Only this time a device had detonated, he'd walked away without a scratch. Well, almost.

Cree held a square of gauze to his forearm as firefighters worked to keep the flames engulfing the old electronics store from spreading to the connected buildings. Echoes of screams and pain threatened to rip reality straight out from under him, and that undeniable guilt he'd tried to bury clawed up his throat.

"That's a pretty nasty gash on your arm. You going to make it?" Alma's voice penetrated through the darkness and planted him firmly back in Battle Mountain.

Relief slammed the lid on the box he'd shoved to the back of his mind. Time caught up with perception. He'd gotten Thorp and Alma out in time. This wasn't Loveland. This wasn't the case that had sent him into hiding. Dark brown eyes centered in his vision, and for a split second, he forgot about why he was here in the first place.

Cree pushed his weight from against the hood of the car. He pried the gauze from his arm, scanning the laceration spanning the underside of his forearm. The bleeding had already slowed. It might need stitches, but EMTs were already busy enough as it was. He wasn't going to keep them from their work. "Mr. Thorp told me he suffered a similar wound in the exact same spot about fifteen years ago when some punk teenager played a prank on him at the store. Something to do with a broken antenna and a lesson in velocity."

A laugh escaped that iron control she seemed to thrive on. Alma settled beside him, surveying the remains of the electronics store that had obviously played a large role in her life growing up here in town. "I remember that day. Mrs. Thorp—Maliya— made me a whole plate of brownies afterward. With walnuts, no less. She thought it was funny as hell when he told her about what had happened. She couldn't stop laughing." She slid one hand beneath his arm and rolled his elbow. "Guess this makes me bad luck."

"I'd hate to think of whatever else I have coming for me if that's true." The pain receded under her touch, a trick of his own mind after living through the latest threat, but he'd take advantage of it anyway. The brain had a funny way of working like that, pretending it hadn't survived a trauma by focusing on something comforting. Something warm. He motioned toward the old man armed with an oxygen mask strapped over his face. Less than twelve hours ago, Alma had been in the same position. He wasn't sure what to think about that. "How's he doing?"

Alma pulled back, and his skin grew cold. She hefted herself on to the damaged car hood, her boots hitting against rusted metal. "He's in shock. And blaming himself for not noticing there was a bomb in his store. I keep telling him he's nuts, but it doesn't make a difference. His wife is on her way."

"That's a true soldier, right there. We take the blame for everything." Cree straightened. Hints of smoke and moisture drove deep into his lungs. "I'm sorry about his store, though. There aren't enough of these places around anymore. Family-owned stores and shops. Hate to see one go, but I'm glad you two got out in time."

"Thanks to you." She knocked one boot into his shin, then focused on the blackened, crumbling structure. "Insurance will pay for any damages as soon as the department releases the store as a crime scene. The Silverton bomb squad is still busy at the primary scene, but they've got a tech waiting for the fire crew to get the flames under control. I'm sure she'll want to get your statement."

Cree pressed his injured arm to his shirt. "It was the same bomber."

His pulse double-timed the longer she didn't answer, and he ripped his attention from the blast site back to her.

"You're sure?" The color had left her face, and there was an undeniable waver to her voice. Spits of hose water plastered against her face and caused the thin hairs near her ears to stick. She scrubbed one hand down her face, and he caught sight of the darkening skin around her arm. A perfect five-fingered bruise.

Hell. He'd been so focused on getting her and Thorp out of there after he'd found the device at the back of the store that he hadn't given a second thought to grabbing her. Only now he realized how hard he must've gripped her arm. "The device was built exactly as you described it, down to the placement of the same coiled, red wire leading from the circuit board to the explosive on the left side. It was C4. Two bricks. Not exactly easy to come by. By the time I saw it, there wasn't time to try to disarm it." He turned to face her as a void of fresh guilt carved through him. "Alma, about that bruise—"

"Officer Gregson, I hear we have you to thank for the lack of bodies this time." Chief Ford tipped his hat in greeting. The department head, whom Cree had pegged to be in his midthirties, was closely followed by a man that could've been Weston Ford's twin. Maybe slightly older.

A day's worth of beard growth shadowed the sharp angles of Easton Ford's jaw and chin. Two distinct lines deepened between his eyebrows as he closed one eye against the afternoon sun to survey the scene. Penetrating deep blue eyes locked on Cree, and the hairs on the back of his neck stood on end. There was something different about this Ford compared to the chief, something worn—battle-tested—and in that moment, Cree recognized a fellow military man. Only this one had obviously seen horrors Cree couldn't begin to imagine.

Chief Ford nodded to Alma. "Majors."

Alma straightened a bit taller, only the tug of her lower lip revealing the pain she must still be feeling from the first blast. She hung both thumbs from her belt. "Chief."

"Hell of a way to start your shift, Alma. Two bombings in a twelve-hour period." Easton Ford twisted, that sharp gaze following the movements of every man and woman on scene. He hiked the sleeves of his red-and-black flannel shirt higher, revealing tanned skin and white scar tissue. "Can't be a coincidence."

"Go big or go home, I suppose, sir." She held her head high, unwilling to let any of them read past her guarded expression, but Cree had dealt with enough victims and witnesses in blasts like this. She couldn't hide from him. "Cree was able to get a visual on the device before it detonated. If it weren't for him, Dr. Pascale would have a lot more bodies on her hands."

"Same design. Most likely the same bomber. There were only fifteen seconds left on the countdown by the time I came across it. Not enough time to defuse and clear the building." Cree said. "Thorp doesn't remember anyone buying the components we described and we lost his receipts somewhere in the blast, but there's no way the perp would've known we'd come here next. They chose this location for a reason, and considering the device was set at the same desk as Thorp's security surveillance system,

I'm betting they realized he had footage of them buying what they needed for the attack at the gulch."

"And came back to ensure we'd never get our hands on it." Chief Ford scratched at the thickening hair down his jaw, one hand set against his hip. "This bomber obviously isn't concerned about hurting people, which makes them even more dangerous. And now that Thorp's surveillance system has been destroyed, we have no idea how many other devices our bomber planned to build." The chief rocked his weight back on one foot. "What were the two of you doing here in the first place, Majors? I sent you home to take it easy for the next few days. You know, considering you almost got blown up. Now I find you at not one but two bombing scenes. It's a miracle you're still alive."

Alma's gaze flickered to Cree's. "Yes, sir. I asked Officer Gregson to help me get a lead on the victim's identity. The lab won't be able to pull anything from the shard of bone left after the first bombing for another week, and the Silverton squad is focused on the device itself. She was all alone in that gulch. Someone out there doesn't know she's missing. I wanted to identify her for the sake of her family and friends."

Frustration contorted the chief's expression as Easton Ford laughed before turning his back on them. "Officer Gregson, please excuse us."

The urge to argue slithered up his throat, but Cree had no business telling Battle Mountain's police chief

how to run his department. As much as he believed
Alma had made the right choice in trying to identify
the victim, she'd obviously ignored her commanding
officer's orders by going after this thing herself. He
noted the embarrassment in Alma's body language
and extracted himself from the conversation a few
yards away.

Alma's nods, the chief's soundless enquiries and
Easton Ford's occasional input were all he was able
to make out over the roar of the fire hoses, but it was
enough to charge the defiance building in his chest.
He wasn't sure what Alma had been running from
all this time, but it was obvious she needed this job.
He couldn't let her take the fall for what'd happened,
and with his record already tarnished, absorbing the
blame wouldn't change a damn thing for him. Cree
strode back toward the threesome, water sprinkling
across his neck and chest. "Chief, listen, I understand
Officer Majors made a mistake in investigating this
case on her own, but—"

"Settle down, Gregson, and keep arguing." Easton
Ford secured a hand over Cree's shoulders, a little
too tight. "I don't know what kind of department
you work for, but that's not how we do things around
here."

Keep arguing?

"I don't understand." He searched her expression,
noting the slight lift at one corner of her mouth. His
own brand of embarrassment clawed up his neck

and into his face. He'd been played. Whatever this conversation was, it hadn't been for his benefit. But someone else's. "You're not being reprimanded, are you?"

"No, but I appreciate your gesture to interfere, all the same." Alma threaded one hand through her hair. "We're taking note of who's watching the scene. I believe the bomber attached the first device to the victim to keep us from identifying her. They didn't want any evidence to survive. By letting the Silverton bomb squad take the lead in the investigation and making it look as though I've been taken off the case, I can stay under the radar while I find out who she was. Maybe then we'll have a lead on who made the bombs and why."

He didn't have to fake the shock overwhelming his control. "She's a rookie, Ford, and you want her to run her own investigation into a bomber who's already set off two devices and killed someone? Without support of the department. Without backup."

"Not exactly," she said. "You're coming, too."

Chapter Four

They'd fooled Cree enough to make him believe she'd been removed from the case.

But had the ploy been enough for a killer?

Her training in bombs had been short but memorable. According to the study of a dozen investigations over the course of the past decade, it was common for bombers to stick around the scene of a crime to watch their handiwork unfold. Sometimes that obsession narrowed on the spread of flames as an arsonist would, or to watching a building crumble in on itself. Other times, it was to take pleasure in how many people had been hurt or killed.

If that was the case, this time the bomber would be disappointed.

Cree had pulled both her and Mr. Thorp from the small store before the explosion, and now they had a chance to get the answers they needed to find the person responsible. He settled against the stucco edging her apartment front door. "You'll have to go about your life as though nothing has changed. Stick to your routine whenever possible. Grocery shopping on Mondays, going for runs around town twice a week. No changes. Understand? We don't want to give the bomber any reason for turning his attention to you."

He'd memorized her routine. Just as she had his. But had it been because of some deep-rooted survival or mere curiosity? Alma shoved the key to her first dead bolt into position and twisted. She wasn't sure which answer she preferred. She followed up with the next dead bolt and the third. Awareness chased down the length of her neck as Cree pushed away from the wall. Three dead bolts hadn't come standard with her lease, and he was too good a cop not to notice. She tightened her grip around the doorknob, the metal instantly warming under her skin. "Someone's been doing their homework."

"Not much else around here to do but people-watch." He backed off a foot, and another shot of shame pooled at the base of her spine. He wasn't going to ask her about the dead bolts. He wasn't going to ask her what Mr. Thorp had meant when he'd called her Dr. Ortega. He wasn't going to put her in a position to explain. Because he knew. That was why he was giving her space right now. He knew, and she couldn't take the weight of seeing one more person in her life face her with pity in their gaze. "Mr. Heinz from downstairs thinks I don't know he's the one who steals the cookies Mrs. Faris leaves for me on my doormat, but one of these days, I'm going to catch him in the act."

Nervous energy skittered down her spine as she considered whether or not she should invite him inside. On one hand, the survivor in her hated the idea of letting a practical stranger into her space, of exposing herself to him. On the other, it would look suspicious if she didn't at least try to pretend the reason they'd be spending time together was because of mutual attraction and not working together to uncover the victim's identity. Pressure built behind her sternum as he waited for her to open the door, and her mouth dried. She didn't have the strength or the patience for mind games she didn't understand how to play. Alma removed her hand from the doorknob and faced him. "I don't want to invite you inside." She hadn't meant the words to burst from her mouth, but it was too late. "Wow. That was a lot harsher than I intended."

Surprise registered across his handsome features as he slid his hands into his jeans. "I understand."

"No. I don't think you do. I just… I don't do this a lot. Talk to people, I mean. I've never had people over, and I don't visit with neighbors, but we're supposed to work together on this case, and I don't know how to…do that." She'd hit her head in the bombing. Yes, that was it. Because this version of herself didn't exist until she'd faced the possibility of him coming inside. She folded her arms across her chest, a classic defensive maneuver he'd spot a mile away. "Simply speaking."

"I don't know if you know this, but you may have chosen the wrong career. Ninety-nine percent of police duty is talking to people." His laugh bubbled past full lips she hadn't taken the time to notice the past few hours. Mainly because the threat of dying had been more of a priority, but now she noted the slight thinning at one side of his mouth compared to the other. A perfect flaw that only made him more real than the fantasy she'd constructed in her head. "Would it help if I asked why you have three dead bolts on your door when every other apartment in this complex has one, including mine?"

He had noticed. Her stomach twisted. His words filtered through her mind, tripping over one another before her heart rate settled at the base of her throat. "Actually, yes. If we're going to work together, I'd rather you talk to me directly than to assume you know me or what I've been through."

Cree ducked his chin. "Mr. Thorp called you Dr. Ortega. I'm guessing Ortega is your maiden name and that you had a completely different life before you found yourself in the middle of a blast zone last night."

"Majors is my married name." An ache settled around her arm, but she didn't have the willpower to pull her attention from the man in front of her. Seemed everywhere she looked these past few weeks, Cree had been there. In the corridor as she brought home groceries, in the diner she frequented nearly every day, at the scene last night. He'd slipped into her life as quietly as a shadow and set up residence just as quickly. "I keep it to remind me what I'm working toward. I was an archaeologist before I signed on with the department."

"Alma Ortega. Wait, the Alma Ortega?" Recognition flared in his expression, and where her first instinct had once been to hold her head high, a part of her now shrank at her two lives converging. "I've read your work. Your discovery of a buried Teotihuacán citadel in the middle of Maya has to be one of the biggest Mexican archaeological finds recorded in over a hundred years."

Excitement bled into his eyes, and her heart practically skipped a beat. "It was." Remnants of that day still played through her mind. Where her colleagues had been so determined to reveal Egyptian and Viking secrets, she and her team had shoved Mexico back into the light. Right where it belonged. She'd never been prouder in her life. There'd been new job offers to teach at universities across the country, television interviews, papers to collaborate on with peers she'd idolized all through her career, and funding to continue her research, but the spotlight, it seemed, had shone too brightly. At least in her case.

"I remember a lot of media coverage from around that time." The light in his gaze dulled. "You disappeared after that. The reigning theory was you'd retired." Cree's attention slipped to the dead bolts behind her. "But that's not what happened, was it?"

She cleared her throat of emotion, but Alma had known this day would come. One that would force her to confront the truth, that would strip her bare and expose her to the world as the coward she'd always known she was. "No. It's not." She rolled her lips between her teeth and bit down to keep herself in the moment, just as she'd been taught to do. Grounding, her therapist had called it. "It's not well known, but my, uh, husband—ex-husband—was also an archaeologist. We worked in the same field, but our focuses were very different. He'd gone the way of Egyptian study in hopes of uncovering the next great King Tut, and I followed my heart to Mexico. After my findings went public and I published, he wasn't thrilled with the attention."

"You mean the attention you were getting," Cree said. "He saw it as a betrayal."

A humorless laugh escaped past her control. It had taken her months to put that puzzle together, and Cree had solved it in minutes. "He changed. Practically overnight. It was so fast I didn't even see it coming. He was so…angry, and the only way he could control it was by directing it at me. By the time I realized the pain wasn't going to stop, that him taking his anger out on me wasn't just jealousy, he'd already isolated me from my colleagues. The job offers had stopped coming in, the phone wasn't ringing and my funding for future research had been allocated to other researchers. My career vanished in the blink of an eye while I was just trying to make it through most nights."

"But you did. Make it through." Cree's shoulders tipped forward as though he had the urge to close the distance between them, but she wasn't sure she could handle that. Not yet. Not with her nerves at an all-time high, and not out here in the middle of their apartment complex corridor. "You left. You walked away. You remade your life and started again."

"Yes." Her voice deadpanned as the memories of her last night in the emergency room threatened to overtake the present. She kicked at a stray pebble under her boots, the edges catching on the underside of her heel. "Much to the disappointment of Mr. Thorp, unfortunately. He always had big dreams for me."

"You know as well as I do, just in the short amount of time I've known him, that man will never be disappointed in you." Cree nodded to her arm, and she craned her chin down. "I'm sorry about the bruise. After I saw the countdown on the timer on that device, the only thing I could think of was to get you out of there. I wasn't thinking about how tight I was holding onto you."

The ache spread around her bicep as she inspected the dark five-fingered bruise. Her heart shuddered at her body's ability to take everything it had been through. This would be just another chapter of that story. Only, this time, she had the choice of how it ended. "You don't have to apologize. If it hadn't been for you, I wouldn't be worrying about anything at all."

"I guess that's true, but I'm still going to apologize." His lopsided smile drove straight past the pressure behind her chest and relieved the valve she'd sealed off what seemed like forever ago. Cree pointed toward his apartment. "I'm going to grab those cookies before Mr. Heinz gets to them first and give you some time to recover. I'll come by tomorrow so we can start looking into your victim. Around eight?"

"Eight is good." Her skin heated as though she'd just made a date with the handsome neighbor across the hall, which, really, she had.

He maneuvered past her, sure to keep his distance, then stopped. "And, Alma, whatever happens with this case, I'll have your back. I give you my word."

MORNING HADN'T COME soon enough. Not for him.

Cree balanced the recycled drink carrier containing two coffees with one hand and knocked lightly on her door with the other while clutching the research he'd printed off last night. Footsteps echoed from inside a split second before the door swung open. Hints of meat, onions and peppers hit him square in the face, and his stomach kicked into overdrive. He'd been up at the crack of dawn and had dived straight into the case. With nothing more than a shard of bone to identify their victim, they had a lot of work ahead of them. So much, in fact, he'd forgotten to eat.

"Hey. Hope I'm not early." He stretched to check his watch, nearly tipping their coffees onto the cement.

"Actually, you're right on time, but I'll be honest. I got a bit of a head start last night after you left." She clutched the edge of the door, craning her head back into what looked like a barely furnished living room and wall-to-wall bookshelves. The same tension he'd noted in her neck and shoulders last night solidified. They'd agreed to work this case together, but the hesitation of inviting him inside hadn't lessened over the course of the past twelve hours. And, hell, after what she'd told him last night, he couldn't blame her. And he wouldn't push her.

"Why don't you wrap whatever you're cooking to go, and we can use the picnic tables in the courtyard to go over the plan," he said. "It'll play into the ruse, right? Us having breakfast together. Besides, it's nice enough we won't overheat for a couple of hours."

"Okay." Relief punctured through the hardened tendons running the length of her delicate neck. She disappeared inside, the door automatically swinging shut. Within thirty seconds, she backed out of the apartment, her hands full of paperwork and two paper plates filled with food. He shifted his load to one hand and held out the other to help, careful not to get too close. Alma glanced up at him with deep, rich brown eyes and a weak smile as she surrendered one of the plates. "Thank you. I wasn't sure if you eat breakfast, but I made Mexican rice with poached eggs."

"Smells delicious." His stomach knotted at the second hit of spices, cheese and sausage.

"Family recipe from my aunt Ramona." She locked all three dead bolts behind her before facing him. "I tend to cook when I'm stressed, and then I eat everything I've made, and I feel better."

"Stressed is an understatement. Getting caught in the middle of a case like this your first week on the job is definitely not for the weak of heart." They moved as one down the length of the corridor and into the open stairwell. The concrete steps and steel handrails vibrated with their descent. "Most people, trained or not, would be curled up in the fetal position right now if they'd survived two explosions. Not agreeing to run a secret investigation into the identity of our victim, let alone cooking breakfast."

"If my history has taught me one thing, it's that I never was good at knowing what was best for me." Her laugh countered the apprehension growing behind his rib cage. Alma settled her plate and the file she'd put together on the old wood planks that passed for a picnic table in the center of their complex. She slid long, lean legs between the tabletop and bench.

The denim jacket she'd donned guaranteed a heat overdose combined with her dark jeans and black T-shirt, but it worked as a prime example of her survival techniques. He imagined that with every bruise she'd sustained during her marriage, she'd learned to hide the truth from the people who cared about her. Friends, family, neighbors, colleagues. She just hadn't broken the habit. Alma nodded toward the file in his hand as he took his seat opposite her. "I take it I'm not the only one who got a head start on this case."

"Uh, no. You're not." He pulled a corn tortilla—handmade from scratch, from what he could tell—out of the mess of rice, meat and peppers on his plate and took a bite. Egg yolks broke across the mountain of comfort food, and he practically melted back in his seat. "Damn, this is good. Where'd you learn how to cook like this?"

"Growing up, my family always had dinner together on Sundays. Everyone would bring something different, and we'd throw it on this massive table that barely fit in our house like a buffet. We'd sit and talk and eat for hours together, sharing our lives and telling jokes." Alma severed eye contact as she focused on her own plate of food and scooped a bit into her mouth. One corner of her mouth tugged into a smile. "My *abuela* insisted I learn to cook just as my mother had. Hands-on. So every Sunday, she'd come over a couple hours early, have me pick out a recipe to cook, and she'd teach me. I was barely big enough to see over the counter, but we made it work. By the time I was six, I could make anything I set my mind to."

"That all sounds great." A twinge of envy slipped between his thoughts as he easily envisioned a smaller version of the woman in front of him surrounded by nothing but love and food and heritage. How had it all gone wrong? "And loud."

"It could be. The police might've been called whenever my uncles and *abuelo* argued about who could burp the loudest." Pure joy replaced the tempest in her eyes as she took another bite of breakfast. "Did you come from a large family, too?"

"Ah, no." He focused on counting each individual grain of rice he could see at the edge of his plate. "I was an only kid. Parents both had military careers. One or both of them would always be on tour."

"You were alone?" The sadness in his voice gutted him straight down to the bone.

"Not all the time." His fingers tingled for a distraction. Something to carve or a leaf to tear through. "If both of my parents were called to active duty, I'd spend that time with my grandfather. He had a cabin out here on the other side of the lake. At first, I hated it. We'd hike all day, fish for our meals and hunt the land to stock up for winter. There were no other kids around. The old man didn't believe in public schools. He homeschooled me even past my eighteenth birthday. Said the best thing I could do for myself and my family was get a real education. None of that 'state-approved nonsense.' After a while, I didn't mind spending time with him. He taught me how to work with my hands, gave me confidence to take care of myself even under the most dire circumstances." A heaviness cemented him in his seat. "But after he died, I just felt alone. I ended up joining the army. My parents were still committed. Figured I might as well fall into the family legacy."

"Where are they now? Your parents?" she asked.

"Major General Gregson and Colonel Gregson just hit thirty years together." Cree pushed back his plate, not able to take another bite. "They are comfortably situated in Washington, DC, advising how to avoid going to war and preparing for it at the same time."

"Wow. Legacy is right." Alma set down her tortilla topped with sausage, rice and onions. She rubbed her hands together before turning her attention to the file she'd built overnight. "You said your grandfather has a cabin on the other side of the lake. To what do we owe the pleasure of your company here at Crescent Ridge Apartments?"

His laugh escaped before he had a chance to second-guess it. "Well, when you put it that way... Truth is, there isn't much to go back to. Once he was gone, I joined up, and the place went to hell over the years. There wasn't anybody here to take care of it. The vegetation started reclaiming the interior and working through the windows. The garden we'd planted together was picked over too many times. All of the appliances stopped functioning. There wasn't really anything left to save."

"I know that area. There aren't too many cabins out there. Both the chief and Easton have a ranch out that way. Whispering Pines. They recently started a veteran rehabilitation center on the land south of the main cabin. I've been helping on the weekends for the past few months between therapy appointments." She took a sip from her coffee, those equally dark eyes settling on his. "Is that why you're here in Battle Mountain? To clean up your grandfather's place?"

If he was being honest with himself, he hadn't even thought of going out there. The connection he'd had to this place, to his grandfather, had died with the old man. Cree wedged his thumbnail between the worn slats of the picnic table. Yet when the guilt and the shame and the weight of the past had started suffocating him from the inside, Battle Mountain was the first place he'd thought of to run to. Not out of any duty to his grandfather but because this place was the only familiarity he had left. This small mining town had created a distinct separation between his new life and the old one, and he wasn't sure he ever wanted to go back.

"I'm sorry. I didn't mean to pry. You don't… You don't have to tell me anything." Alma wrapped both of her hands around her to-go coffee cup and shook her head. The corner of her file folder scraped against the aged wood as she pulled it closer and flipped it open. "We should focus on the case."

"No. It's okay." He wanted her to know. Because even after everything that had happened, after everything his grandfather had taken time and energy to teach him, he'd missed that connection. The one people shared. It had been the reason he'd gone into the military, that he'd tried to work his way into his parents' world. It was why he'd responded to the scene of the bomb last night, and why he'd agreed to work with Alma in the first place. It was that connection—not the isolation—that had brought him to this sleepy, nearly dead town. Cree gripped his coffee cup harder than he meant to. "I didn't come here to fix up my grandfather's place, Alma. I came to Battle Mountain to hide."

Chapter Five

"I don't understand." He'd come to hide? Apprehension settled in the deepest recesses of her joints and tightened the tendons down the length of her legs. The kind of people who'd chosen Battle Mountain to hide had brought nothing but death and terror behind them. The chief's fiancée and mother of his unborn child, Dr. Chloe Miles, had narrowly escaped a serial killer who'd tracked her here. And Genevieve Alexander, Easton Ford's significant other, had caught the attention of a violent killer determined to tear apart her life for a case she'd prosecuted years ago.

The people here didn't deserve to live in fear or wonder if they'd wake to find one of their loved ones the center of a homicide investigation. This town had been through enough. How much more were they supposed to take? Then again, she herself was a lure to a violent person if her ex ever decided to look for her. "You said you were with the Larimer County bomb squad. If that's true, what on earth would someone like you have to hide from?"

The edge of the wooden bench dug into the soft underside of her thighs until it was all she could think about through the low ringing in her ears. Her heart rate spiked. She'd trusted her instincts to bring Cree in on this investigation, to work this case beside her, but how long had she let herself stay blind to her ex-husband's darkness? Her stomach weighed heavy with breakfast that threatened to retaliate at any given moment. Alma shifted her weight across the bench as her skin heated.

"More than you know." Cree fidgeted with his coffee cup until he caught himself digging through the recycled material. "Listen, Alma, you were straight with me last night. It took a lot of guts for you to share what you'd been through, but I find it hard to trust people. Seems every time I do, someone ends up hurt."

She leaned forward in her seat, and their breakfast, the investigation, the pain in the back of her shoulder—it all disintegrated until there was only the two of them. "The only person who knows about what happened between me and my ex-husband other than you is Easton Ford." Her mouth dried. "Not the chief. Not my parents or the rest of my family. As far as they're concerned, my ex left me to make his own mark in the archaeological world."

"Why would you lie?" Surprise broke through Cree's guarded expression. "Why not tell them the truth?"

"Because I was afraid of how disappointed they'd be in me. The last time I was in the house we'd shared, I ended up in the emergency room with a shattered wrist, but I was so embarrassed about what was happening, I couldn't go to the clinic here in town. I drove three hours to Alamosa for treatment, sobbing because of the pain. At the time, it seemed worth the risk, but looking back, I wasn't thinking straight. I just wanted the pain to stop, so I went along with whatever story he'd prepared to explain the bruises and cast." Her inhale shuddered. "Easton was the one who found me. He was there with the Alamosa district attorney after they'd closed the case they were working together, but while she was in surgery, he saw me. Somehow, he knew exactly what'd happened, and he offered to help me get out."

She spread her hands out in front of her and pressed into the table to rein in the residual emotion attached to those memories. "My point is you can't get through this life alone. I know what it's like to be surrounded by people and still feel so isolated, but help can come from the most random sources. So if we're going to work this case together, if we're going to have each other's backs, we need to at least be honest. You don't have to tell me your entire history. I just need to know if working with you is going to get me or anyone else in this town hurt."

Cree ducked his head. "You're right. Whoever is setting these devices has already killed one person, and they're not afraid of killing more. We're not going to be able to stop them unless we work together."

A hot breeze mazed through the courtyard and kicked up the sweet scent of freshly cut grass and wildflowers. It combined with the hint of clean soap coming off his skin. Or had her desperation for connection only imagined that part?

"When I told Chief Ford I'm with the Larimer County bomb squad, that was the truth. I'm still technically a tech assigned to that jurisdiction, but I've been on leave for the past eight months." His voice dipped an octave, and goose pimples budded along her arms.

Something had happened eight months ago in Larimer County. He'd obviously been involved, which meant there'd been a threat of some sort. A bomb, maybe. Eight months. Why did that timeline sound so familiar? Nausea clawed up her throat, like something alive, and Alma straightened a bit taller. Regret exploded as she scanned the length of his arms and searched his face. "The bombing at that oil and gas meeting with the board of county commissioners." His gaze met hers head-on, and it was in that moment, she understood. "Loveland. You were there."

"An ecoterrorist group had gotten word about the policy changes the board of county commissioners were considering." The muscles along his jaw ticked in rhythm to the pulse pounding hard at the base of his neck. "By the time emergency crews got through the debris and rubble, three had died. Another half dozen of my team injured. All because I didn't find the device in time."

Despite her efforts to avoid media consumption after her divorce had gone public and the rumors had started breaking through the cracks into her new world, she remembered the coverage that entire week after the bomb had gone off. "You seemed to have walked away without a scratch."

"Just because you can't see them, doesn't mean they aren't there." His eyes glazed for a split second as though he'd become a victim to the past before he seemed to come back to himself. To her. Cree pushed the file he'd brought with him across the table. "As for this case, Silverton's squad will already have pulled a list of similar incidents in the area from the NCIC database. It's common for bombers to detonate practice devices and build up courage before the big event, so I reached out to a friend working for the ATF to search incident reports in this area going back six months that used the same kind of setup we saw. That way, the inquiry doesn't lead back to our investigation."

"Did your contact find anything?" She pried open the manila folder and set her hand over the papers inside to keep the wind from ripping them away.

"Colorado State Patrol responded to complaints filed by two different hikers concerning what sounded like dynamite charges being set off out-side of Ouray three weeks ago." Cree tapped the file in front of her with his index finger, and it was only then she recognized a thin scar trailing from the first knuckle diagonal to the second. The kind of scar that would stay after having a finger reattached after a bombing. "According to the reports, when the troopers got to the area, they found the ground ripped open in several places and fresh evidence of scoring on nearby rocks. They don't have a suspect, but they did find this."

He dug out a page from the back of the file and set it on top of the reports. The photo revealed a cor-ner of a familiar green motherboard component. The same kind that had been used in the bombs both she and Cree had seen with their own eyes. It wasn't im-possible that another bomber had utilized this spe-cific setup to design their creation. But what were the chances of it being so close to Battle Mountain?

"A motherboard." She threaded her fingers under the single photo, a hangnail catching on the reports underneath. "Was anyone hurt in the explosions?"

"No reported fatalities. State Patrol wasn't able to pull any prints from the components or get a de-scription from the hikers who filed the report either." Cree folded his arms across the surface of the old table. "But if this incident is a practice run for our bomber like I think it is, they made a point to avoid

Battle Mountain jurisdiction. Like they were waiting for the right time to strike."

"Or the right someone. Maybe our victim?" Alma set her face in one hand, her elbow digging into the weathered picnic table. One wrong move and a sliver would imbed in her skin, but it was almost preferable compared to the pressure to solve this case. "I've gone through the missing person reports a dozen times. There aren't any victims who fit the description of the woman I found at the bottom of that gulch, but it's possible I'll get a hit off the baby's photo in the locket."

"Good idea." Cree collected the file folder he'd shared with her. "I'm going to head down to the station to get in touch with State Patrol, try to get them to send us any evidence they collected at the scene. If we're chasing our tails, I want to know sooner rather than later." He collected his discarded paper plate then hers and deposited them in the trash set at the end of the expansive table. "Thanks for breakfast. I'll work with you to the end of time if this is the kind of food I can look forward to."

Warmth shot through her as his sincerity solidified between them. Appreciation hadn't ever been a habit of her ex's, and the effect of something so simple lightened the isolation determined to suffocate her from the inside. "You're welcome. Let me know where you get with State Patrol."

"Will do." He nodded once and then headed for

the pickup parked at the back of the shared lot, the muscles down the backs of his thighs flexing beneath the denim that fit him perfectly.

Her own appreciation churned low in her belly as he waved goodbye through the passenger-side window and maneuvered free of the lot. For someone who'd come to Battle Mountain to hide, Cree Gregson had certainly made his mark on this town. And her. She wasn't sure how to explain it, but there was a sense of...safety that came with being the center of the man's attention. Not brittle or dependent as it had been with her ex. But grounding. Supportive even. She couldn't remember the last time she'd felt at home in her own skin, but there was something about Cree that gave her permission to loosen her need for control, that made it easier to breathe.

She headed back upstairs to her apartment and caught sight of a white slip of paper taped to the door. Alma checked the corridor, her hand reaching for the weapon she'd left secured in her safe in the laundry closet. The note hadn't been there before her and Cree's meeting, and she hadn't seen anyone climb the stairs while they'd been in view at the table. She tugged the torn paper free and exposed the unfamiliar handwriting inside. *"Back off, or next time you won't survive."*

CREE SLAMMED THE phone down. "Damn it."

"I take it State Patrol didn't buy your story about

you being a Silverton bomb technician." Macie Barclay, Battle Mountain PD's single dispatcher, office manager and overall redheaded stepchild, set down a mug of coffee at the end of the desk.

"They did not." He threaded his fingers through the mug's handle. "I think I lost them somewhere around not being able to give them my badge number so they could put in the request."

"You've got to put some desperation into it. Like the entire town's future is weighing on your shoulders alone, and you are the only one who can save us." Macie lifted her hands in a dramatic pose as she leaned against the edge of one of many empty desks throughout the station. In an instant, the drama faded, leaving a wide smile across her face. "Oh, you're going to want to watch yourself. Chief Frasier gifted me that mug after he retired a few years ago. Said he made it with his own two hands, but I'm pretty sure he didn't know what the hell he was doing. Gets hotter the longer you wait to drink it."

"Wouldn't know." He hadn't been able to feel much after the bombing last year. His surgeon had done a damn fine job putting everything back where it was supposed to go, but nerve damage was a different beast altogether. Except when it came to Alma. For a moment while he'd helped her get settled at their impromptu breakfast this morning, he could've sworn he'd felt something. Then again, he'd sustained brain trauma during the Loveland bombing when a chunk of concrete had crashed down on top of him during his attempted escape from the building. For all he knew, he'd imagined a lot of things. Like the way she'd flushed when he'd thanked her for breakfast. "When is Chief Ford supposed to get back from his brief with Silverton's bomb squad?"

"Not until this afternoon." The dispatcher took a sip of coffee from her own mug, green eyes far too aware and curious. Straight white teeth and lipsticked lips added to her bohemian-style white dress and midcalf-length cardigan sweater. She curled brightly painted, manicured nails around her mug as full eyebrows drew inward. "Remind me why you can't just tell them who you are and ask with pretty pleases and cherries on top? Please tell me it has something to do with why Easton is covering Officer Majors's shift today."

"It's complicated." Apart from the fact he and Alma had to keep their investigation under the radar, identifying himself as the technician who failed to do his job wouldn't get him far with other agencies. He'd learned that from experience. Suspicion distracted him from laying out a plan to get a look at the evidence State Patrol had gathered at the scene outside of Ouray. Gossip had never been any interest to him. He'd done his homework when he'd come to town. Not only about Battle Mountain's history and its residents but its department. Macie Barclay had been a fixture in this sad excuse for a station long before trouble had reared its ugly head this past year. Going on ten years from what he could tell from her personnel records. He'd trained to pick apart bombers' motives and devices then reassemble them under pressure of saving lives, but his instincts said Macie's interest was purely for entertainment's sake. And hell, he didn't blame her given the quiet isolation of this place. In fact, he was surprised the dispatcher hadn't made hand puppets out of tissues and craft supplies to give her an excuse to talk to herself. He scanned the station for a set of plastic shifty eyes staring back at him. "You known Alma long?"

"First-name basis." Straw-looking sandals ground harder into the industrial carpet as Macie straightened, and an amused edge cut into her expression. "Considering Officer Majors doesn't talk to anyone unless she absolutely has to, I'd say you should be flattered."

His gut kicked hard. "You already know why I didn't tell State Patrol who I am, don't you? This was just a ploy to get me to talk."

"I'm good at reading people." Macie's mouth tugged higher at one side. "Let me give you some advice, Officer Whoever-the-Hell-You-Are."

"Gregson," he said.

Macie laughed, as though his name didn't matter. "You're new in Battle Mountain. From what I've been able to tell from your personnel records, you've only lived in and worked in large cities with the support of an entire organization behind you. Larimer County and the army. Here? We protect our own. We have to. Otherwise this town would've been wiped off the map when the mining companies went bankrupt. Do you understand?"

She'd done her homework, the same as he'd done his, and admiration coiled through him. "You're worried my interest in working with Officer Majors is about more than solving this case and that she might get hurt when the investigation is closed."

"Will she?" Macie took a calm sip of her coffee, too calm. "Because while there might be three official police officers in this department, I can guarantee you I know how to hide bodies better than the serial killers they've brought to justice."

"Is that so?" The threat burrowed under his skin. As much as he wanted to ignore the possibility of ending up as a victim at the hand of the sarcastic, redheaded dispatcher, a thread of truth burned behind her words. "In that case, I'll be sure to watch my step."

"See that you do, Officer Gregson of 7356 2nd Street, apartment 201." Relief loosened the tension in her shoulders as she shrugged. The desk phone rang, and Macie turned on her heels to answer. "Wow. It's been a while since I've threatened someone. I've missed it."

He turned back to the monitor taking up a good chunk of real estate on the old, dilapidated desk, as a shiver raced along his spine. Taking Battle Mountain PD's dispatcher at face value had been a mistake. One he wouldn't make again.

He accessed the national criminal database again and pulled up the State Patrol case. No fatalities. No sign of a suspect. The canines had detected the use of C4 during the scene processing, but there hadn't been any DNA to narrow down the identity of the bomber. Only the recovery of fresh footprints leading to what looked to be ATV tracks. His gut said this was the bomber who'd killed a woman in the bottom of the gulch two nights ago. He just needed something. The timing and the location couldn't be coincidences. From what he'd been able to see of the device in Galaxy Electronics before it detonated, the bomb's designer had built a solid means of destruction. That meant experience with explosives and patience. But where did the bomber get the explosive?

C4 was heavily regulated by the Bureau of Alcohol, Tobacco, Firearms and Explosives. Every company or citizen in possession of the explosive apart from the military or government had to register it with the ATF, but that didn't account for explosives that had been stolen. He read through the rest of the incident report. Since there hadn't been any fatalities, State Patrol hadn't pursued a criminal investigation. They did, however, cue in ATF. Cree opened the Bomb Arson Tracking System run by the bureau and sifted through local incidents from the past six months. The most recent entry detailed the theft of twenty pounds of C4 from a construction site in Ouray. The thief had broken the lock on the secure container in the middle of the night a month ago. "Bingo."

They had the source of the explosive. Now all he needed was something to identify the victim caught in the blast. The tests detonated in the desert outside of Ouray fit the timing, but why had the bomber waited so long to kill their victim? Why here in Battle Mountain? "Maybe you couldn't find her," he said to himself.

Cree recalled Alma's description of the victim. Blond hair, a thin face, Caucasian, tall. Approximately thirty-five years old. Alma had already gone through the missing person reports without any luck, but there was a chance they'd underestimated when their victim had gone missing. Clicking through to the national missing persons database, he set the parameters and extended their time frame to a year. Dozens of faces filled the screen, and his mouth dried in an instant. A dozen women smiling at the camera stared back at him from pixelated photos, most likely saved from social media accounts. He read through their names, but no one on the list jumped out. He'd have to sit Alma down to go through the possibilities. Too many.

Macie penetrated his peripheral vision. She handed him a note, her voice shaking. "That was

Alma on the phone. She didn't want to call in over the radio in case the bomber you're investigating is listening. Something happened at her apartment. I think you better get back home."

His heart thudded hard against his rib cage as he took the note from her. Cree shot to his feet, nearly crumpling the slip of paper in his palm, and raced through the back of the station. He slammed against the glass back door and bolted for his truck across the parking lot. In seconds, Main Street's red brick buildings and green landscaping blurred in his vision as he battled with crossing pedestrians and calm traffic. Sweat built in his hairline and beneath his T-shirt neckline with every scenario that played across his mind. He shouldn't have left her alone. He should've been there.

Burnt rubber and the squeal of tires drowned the sound of his own breathing as he skidded to a stop in the complex's parking lot five minutes later. He ripped free of the truck, his legs burning with every rushed step as he climbed the stairs. Her door swung open as he reached the top step.

Alma flinched back into the doorframe a split second before recognition flared. "Damn it. You scared me."

Cree scanned her for injuries, noting her pressed uniform and the police-issued weapon on her right hip. She was undercover for this investigation, ironically in uniform and business as usual, but something had spooked her enough to armor herself in the time he'd been gone. "Tell me what happened."

"See for yourself." She stepped free of the door-jamb and motioned him inside, but where he'd noted defiance at the primary scene and outside of Galaxy Electronics after the second bombing, now there was uncertainty. "I came upstairs to start running missing person reports on the baby's photo from the locket after you'd gone to the station. I found a note taped to my door. When I got inside, I walked into this."

A small, circular kitchen table had been turned on its side, both chairs in pieces. Glass crunched under his boots as he surveyed the destruction. Every single item she'd possessed had been destroyed as far back as the bedroom at the end of the hall. Pressure built behind his rib cage, and a low ringing filtered through his ears. "You locked the doors before we went down to the courtyard. I watched you."

"Yeah." She studied the carnage of her life and settled her weight against the open front door. "But three dead bolts and an alarm system didn't stop whoever knows I'm working this case."

Chapter Six

A siren blipped from the complex's entrance.

She interlaced her fingers together and pressed the side of her hand into the same table she and Cree had sat at for breakfast this morning as Chief Ford and Easton went through the scene. The distraction wasn't strong enough to neutralize the void. Someone had broken into her apartment, destroyed everything she owned, including her clothes. The only thing to survive had been her gun safe and uniform, which had both been stored in the safe in the laundry closet.

Her cover was already blown.

Whoever had murdered the woman in the gulch hadn't fallen for the theater she and the chief had drummed up after the second bombing. They knew she was still working the investigation and that she'd taken it upon herself to identify the victim, but she wasn't the only one lost in this explosive puzzle.

Easton and Cree's canvass of the complex hadn't turned up anything concrete. Seemed the person who'd left the note on her door and ripped apart the few valuables she'd been able to escape her former life with had gone out of their way to avoid being seen. They'd slipped into her life and out as quickly as the sense of security she'd built here and turned her apartment into a crime scene. Now she didn't know what to do. Or where to go.

"You look like you could use one of these." Cree offered her a large disposable cup, and Alma automatically accepted. Coffee. From his own apartment, from the look of it. His mountainous shoulders she'd been all too tempted to relax into when he'd arrived at her apartment pierced through the haze closing in. He took a seat on the bench beside her, and her boots left the ground for a fraction of a second.

"In that case, I must look like death." She took her first swig and almost melted on the spot. The sharp kick to her senses rocketed her pulse higher in an instant, but along with the clearing fog came an awareness of the man beside her.

"I think it's best if I don't respond to that comment." Cree studied the scene as though trying to commit to memory every nosy neighbor and curious bystander considering jumping the perimeter tape for a closer look. Even Mrs. Faris had hooked her Siamese up to the leash to see what was going on outside her door. "I've gotten myself in trouble before."

The ease with which he joked with her nearly had her choking on the dark master that magically transformed reality with a few good sips. It was all too easy to imagine the two of them teasing like this back and forth over coffee in the mornings, maybe after a night in front of the TV with a coffee table full of Chinese leftovers. "I'll bet you have."

Despite the reprieve from the undercurrent of fear, anger and determination, her laugh died as quickly as it had surfaced. The fantasy dissipated in front of her as she caught sight of Easton and Chief Ford conversing at the base of the stairs that led to her apartment. Because that was all it was. A fantasy. The only reason she'd been targeted by the bomber they were chasing was because she'd become a cop. And the only reason she'd become a cop was to guarantee her safety.

Following whatever this was between her and Cree wasn't safe.

Her apartment wasn't safe.

She didn't feel safe, and without that basic need, there couldn't be anything between them. Her lungs evacuated what little air remained as she set her coffee on the bench.

"I guess the cat's out of the bag." He nodded toward the Ford brothers. "Someone knows you're still working this case."

"From the way those two are looking, I think the cat is dead, and the bag is on fire." Alma noted the frustration in her colleagues' body language. She'd learned to read people real fast during her marriage. It had been a survival technique, a way to prepare for

the worst while hoping for the best. Right now, both
Ford men were trying to avoid her attention to keep
her from seeing their expressions, like she needed
to be protected. Neither had any idea what she'd survived. Easton understood the mechanics, but there
was a difference between seeing the outward damage inflicted on a person and acknowledging the permanent scars inside. "Did State Patrol agree to send
the evidence they have from the incident outside of
Ouray three weeks ago?"

"Not even a little." Cree set his elbows against his
knees, accentuating bulky muscle up his arms and
across his shoulders, and her gut clenched. What
was it about that attractive casing and penetrating
gaze that worked to erode the promise she'd made to
herself to stop accepting people for what they were
at face value? What was it about him? "But through
some grunt work, I'm pretty sure I found the location where the C4 was stolen. A construction site in
Ouray. A month ago."

"Pretty sure?" she asked.

"State Patrol never followed through with a criminal investigation, but the contractor in charge of the
project reported twenty pounds of C4 went missing
to the ATF around the same time those two hikers
called in the incident," he said.

"You believe that's our bomber." Her skin prickled
down the backs of her arms as she followed the curve
of his jaw and patterned a design from the three gray

hairs near his chin. He was handsome. She couldn't deny him that, and the way he'd gone out of his way to give her space, to not push her to give more of herself away, only made him more attractive.

"Makes the most sense. Stealing the explosive, testing it outside of Battle Mountain—no one would've seen this guy coming until it was too late." Cree tugged his phone from his back pocket and slid his thumb up the screen. The device unlocked, revealing a photo of two men standing in a patch of forest. A mere glimpse at the picture revealed a young Cree, likely taken before he'd gone into the military, standing with a much older man. His grandfather, if she had to guess. "There are still a lot of missing pieces, and now with you as a possible target, we have to tread more carefully." He slightly craned his head toward her. "I'm glad you're okay."

His flare of sincerity and concern tunneled through the armor she'd donned every day since walking away from her ex, and straight into bone. The ache in her shoulder lessened the longer he studied her, and a wave of heat simmered beneath her skin. Her fight-or-flight instincts had been triggered countless times over the past year. A sound in the night, a shadow climbing along the wall, even calls from wrong numbers. But despite the threat…she'd never felt safer than she did now, with Cree. But what happened when this investigation was over and they were no longer partners? What happened if he decided to go back to Loveland and pick up the pieces of his own life? She slid one hand into her uniform pocket, running her thumb along the length of the locket's chain. "Whoever did that to my apartment wasn't looking to confront me directly. If they know where I live, they know I'm armed. I don't think they'll try again."

"And if they do?" he asked.

"Well, considering I don't even know where I'm going to sleep tonight, I don't think they'll have any luck tracking me down." She'd meant it as a joke, but reality had popped the small bubble they'd built around themselves the past few minutes. Everything she'd built over the past year was gone. "To be honest, I'm not really sure what I'm supposed to do now."

"How would you feel about crashing at my place?" Cree's voice wavered on the last word, and pure panic exploded through her. He raised his hands in surrender, palms forward, as though he understood exactly why that was such a bad idea. "That wasn't an invitation to… Damn it. I didn't mean… Let me start over." The terror etched into his expression broke through her primal defenses. "I meant you can crash in my apartment, and I'll sleep in my truck."

So this what was he was like on shaky ground. She couldn't say it wasn't amusing. Alma played through her options, each grimmer than his suggestion. "You're cute when you're nervous. I like it." She bumped her uninjured shoulder against his. "Thank you. I appreciate it, and I promise not to go through your dresser drawers or medicine cabinet."

"Well, now I'm worried you will." His laugh triggered a chain reaction starting with air stalling in her lungs and ending with a slight tingling in her toes. It was deep, rough, and engrained itself into her memory without a fight. "Just steer clear of the stuff under the bed. It'll be better for our partnership."

Partnership. That single word had only one meaning when she'd recruited him into this investigation, but now…the possibility for more warmed behind her rib cage. Over the course of two days, the connection between them had evolved from an emotionally detached plan to solve this case to the possibility of friendship. Maybe more. It was that last thought that should've terrified her. She'd been so blind to the rage inside of her ex-husband. She'd fallen victim to the romantic gestures, feigned support and the mask he'd hidden behind just for her. But something she couldn't identify promised Cree was exactly as he presented to the world. Perceptive to what she needed. Defensive against any possible threat. Capable of handling the baggage she carted behind her. She could only imagine how good it would feel to have that support all the time. "I give you my word. I will not go through the stuff under your bed."

That forest green gaze she'd come to trust lingered on her for a series of breaths. His phone vibrated with an incoming message, and it took everything she had to sever eye contact. "I had Macie forward me photos of missing women matching the description you gave me of the victim, going back a year. We've been so focused on believing the bombing was a spur-of-the-moment opportunity for our killer, but I'm starting to believe this has been a long time coming." He handed off his phone. "Any of these women look familiar?"

Alma scrolled down the entries, studying each face carefully before moving to the next. Every muscle in her body contracted as she reached the last photo in the lineup. She turned the screen to face him. "That's her."

It was a perfect match. The woman's hair was a bit longer in the photo, maybe a hint darker than Alma remembered under the circumstances, but the same almond-shaped eyes stared back at her. The same laugh lines carved from the widest part of her nose to the edges of her full mouth. The same necklace accentuated the woman's neck.

"You're sure?" Cree asked.

Alma shoved to her feet. She tugged the locket she'd recovered at the scene from her pocket and let Cree compare the one in her hand to the one around the woman's neck in the photo. There wasn't an ounce of doubt in her body. "Our victim's name is Erica Harmon."

THEY HAD A NAME.

The missing person report had been filed by Travis Foster, either a concerned friend or family member of the victim. If anyone could tell them why Erica Harmon had come to Battle Mountain or what she'd been running from, it was him. His driver's license had popped with an Ouray address, and Cree maneuvered the truck down Red Mountain Pass toward the San Juan town as Alma reviewed the man's background information and personal records. Anything to give them a connection to their victim. "Navigation puts us about ten minutes out."

She shifted in her seat, her arm sling scratching against the truck's window controls. "Too bad. I think I might miss the numbness in my glutes." Gravity increased its hold as he took the next curve, and Alma's upper body crossed the midline of the cabin. The weight of her attention tightened the space between his shoulder blades. "All those times you've gotten yourself in trouble for saying the wrong thing… Was there someone in particular doling out the punishment?"

Sunlight cut through the windshield as he curved around the road. Steel guardrails separated jagged gray rocks and wild grass from asphalt, with dense green trees staggering up the side of the mountain. The one-lane road curved and switch-backed along the pass to drag out the quick descent into the valley, but Cree couldn't deny he'd grown comfortable with the woman in the passenger seat. Or that he was looking forward to the return trip. "Is that your way of asking me if I'm single?"

"I just noticed you haven't had a lot of visitors the past few months. Other than Mrs. Faris," she said.

"What makes you think she and I aren't an item?" He flashed her a wide smile. "She doesn't bake cookies for just anyone, you know."

"Let me guess. You fell in love on those long walks with her cat." Her laugh punctured through the last of his hesitation. Free of external threats and influences these past two hours, Alma had lost the tension in her shoulders and her determination to hide behind that guarded expression. Instead, they'd talked about their mutual compulsion to learn new skills, read rather than watch television and stay physically fit for all situations. Even planned to take a run together one of these mornings. It had been nice. Comfortable. Despite her former life as an archaeologist, Alma was turning out to be more cop than he'd estimated. She was one of the most committed and loyal officers he'd worked with. Who else would've taken the responsibility of identifying a victim of a bombing when the entire investigation had been prioritized to stopping a bomber first and foremost? Hell, because of her he'd landed himself right back in the middle of an investigation, and he didn't hate it. He'd handled the most delicate, explosive components during his stretch as a bomb tech, but his partner came with a very different set of instructions. She set her uninjured hand on his thigh. "No, wait. I've got a better one. You fought for her when Mr. Heinz from downstairs challenged you to a duel for her hand."

"You think you're being funny, but that old guy hits harder than you might think. My jaw still clicks every time I yawn. Although our duel involved fighting for cookies and not to win over the heart of a seventy-year-old single retiree." Cree recalled all the instances he'd gone out for his morning run to find a plateful of baked goods wrapped in cellophane. "Wait. Now that I think about all the stuff she's baked for me, does Mrs. Faris really think we're dating?"

"Look at it this way," Alma said. "It'll only be for another twenty years or so. If that, considering how much of her own baking she eats."

"She does make a mean pie." He couldn't remember the last time he'd laughed like this. Faster than he'd intended, the valley opened up in front of them through the windshield. Their laughter died at the realization, and Alma removed her hand from his thigh, leaving a solid print of heat behind. Cree cleared his throat to bring himself back into the moment, but it had been a good reprieve these past couple of hours. "We're getting close."

Ouray took pride in regarding itself as the Switzerland of America and the outdoor recreational capital of Colorado. Rugged peaks guarded the small town that had an even smaller population than Battle Mountain, and its colorful roofs brightening a grid-like layout made it a perfect choice for a holiday or a vacation postcard. From the east boundary of the town, it didn't take them long to find Travis Foster's town house, nestled between two just like it. Cree parked along the curb. Plain beige siding stretched horizontally across the building with a bright blue door, the garage sporting the same look. White trim outlined three windows at the front but failed to add any personality to the home itself. "Doesn't look like much."

Cree shouldered out of the truck at the sight of the Ouray Police Department cruiser pulling up in front of them. Alma rounded the hood to catch up. Her courtesy call to Ouray police had been met with frustration and defiance. Towns this small went out of their way to make sure they avoided stepping on one another's toes, but there hadn't been time to convince the local police chief they had a solid lead. Hell, they didn't even have a body. Cree nodded to the sergeant adjusting his hat as he climbed from the vehicle.

"Sergeant Hale, thanks for coming out." Alma stretched her hand in greeting. "Your chief told us you'd be joining us."

"Officer Majors, I presume." The six-foot officer dressed in navy blues and a bright gold shield on his chest hiked his thumbs under his belt. The ten-gallon hat cast shadows across a lean, square, middle-aged face with nondescript features. A man of few words.

Cree could get along with a guy like that. Then again, the sergeant seemed to be making it a point to let them know he and Alma weren't welcome. "Chief told me you're here to talk to one of our residents in your bombing, but I'll be the one asking the questions here. Travis Foster doesn't have a criminal record and is just trying to get through most days as a single father. He's well-liked, especially considering how many jobs his company provides this town, and I won't have you accusing him of having had something to do with your investigation."

"Sergeant, we have no intention of accusing anyone." Alma dismissed the clear-cut hostility from the Ouray officer and retracted her offered hand. "We just want to ask him about the woman he filed a missing person report for."

"You're talking about Erica," Sergeant Hale said.

"You knew her?" Cree asked.

Hale diverted his attention to the town house. "I've been telling him for months she up and left because of the pressure of being a mom. My own wife went through the same thing after our second kid. Postpartum depression, the doctor said. Didn't take it seriously at first. I mean, most women do just fine after delivering their babies, but the more you think about it, the more you see the signs something isn't right."

"And Erica was showing those signs leading up to her disappearance?" Alma's gaze narrowed.

"The last time I saw her before she hightailed it out of here, she was in my station asking questions about a restraining order. I'd never seen her so…" Sergeant Hale shifted his weight into one leg. "Gaunt, paranoid even. I had half a mind to call Travis to come get her, but she ran out of there so fast I lost her before I'd even gotten to the door. When Travis came in to file the missing person report a few days later, I asked him about it. He swears everything had been fine between her and the baby, and that something else had her spooked. To be honest, after all these months she's been gone, I'm starting to believe him."

Gaunt. Paranoid. Restraining orders. Hell, it sounded as though Erica Harmon had been pushed to the edge and was trying to do whatever it took from keeping herself going off the deep end. Cree's attention slid to Alma, and his stomach dropped. Everything Hale had just described could fit postpartum depression. Or an abusive relationship. "Did Ms. Harmon tell you who she wanted to get a restraining order against?"

"No." Hale shook his head. "Seems she wasn't exactly happy with my answers, didn't like the idea a piece of paper wasn't enough to keep someone from breaking the order or that the offender could be back on the street within twelve to twenty-four hours."

Alma rolled her head forward a hair's breadth, a simple enough action, but one that spoke volumes. At least to him. She cleared her throat. "Public records didn't show any record of a marriage, but you said Erica and Travis have a child together, is that right?"

"Common-law marriage. Those kids have been together as long as I've known them, since high school. Always thought they'd make it. Guess I was wrong." Hale headed for the bright blue front door and pounded his fist against the wood. "Travis, it's Gary. Just need a couple minutes of your time."

Gravel crunched under Cree's boots as he maneuvered closer to the door, his awareness of his partner at an all-time high. Their victim had gone to a police station and started asking about a restraining order. That, coupled with the paranoia, would've triggered Alma's defenses. Not only was she trained to spot it, Alma had lived it, too, but for the life of him he couldn't read what was going on behind those brown eyes.

The door swung inward, and a version of the man they'd run a background check on centered himself in the doorway. A toddler, who Cree guessed was around a year or year and a half, squeezed chubby thighs on either side of Travis's hip and stared out at them with two fingers in his mouth. "Hey, Gary. I wasn't expecting you until tomorrow." Travis nodded a greeting before his attention targeted Alma and then Cree. Color drained from the man's face as he took in Alma's uniform, and he clutched his son tighter. "What's going on?"

"Travis, we're here about Erica." Hale removed his hat and fiddled with it between both hands. "This here is Officer Majors and Cree Gregson from Battle Mountain. They believe they may have found your wife."

Chapter Seven

Her heart had lodged in her throat. There didn't seem to be enough air out here in the great outdoors as she studied the toddler staring straight back at her. It was him, the baby from the locket. She could see the similarities in his wide eyes—the same as his mother's—in the way his nose bubbled at the edges and the shape of his mouth. The photo she'd clung to for the past three days didn't compare to the handsome boy laying his head against his father's shoulder.

Alma forced her hand to her side instead of giving in to the urge to tug the keepsake from her pocket. They'd found the victim's family, but the hollowness that had carved through her that first time she'd been on the receiving end of her ex-husband's rage warned that the person who'd killed Erica Harmon was standing right in front of them.

"What do you mean 'may have'? Either you found her, or you didn't." Travis Foster ran his palm up the length of the toddler's spine. He threw his frantic questions to Alma, and her gut seized up. "Where is she? Is she safe? Can I see her?"

Her pulse thickened behind her ears.

"Travis, let's go inside before the neighbors start eavesdropping." Hale reached a single hand out and gripped Foster by the shoulder, maneuvering him back into the small town house.

Alma and Cree followed suit as the pressure intensified at the back of her skull.

Beige paint and tan floor-to-ceiling tile darkened the interior of the town house. Two separate cat towers took up a good amount of space as they stepped down into the sunken living room. Sunlight cut through the single window at the back of the main level and gleamed off a small, circular dining room set. Toys, clothing and stains added to the crowded feeling throughout as Foster turned to face them.

"You'll have to excuse the mess. Erica was usually the one to keep things organized." Foster bounced the toddler in his arms in front of what looked like an old, disassembled computer. No evidence of a motherboard inside. "I filed a missing person report for Erica six months ago. Where is my wife?"

Cree took up position at her right side, and the wash of anxiety that had nearly pulled her under lessened. "Mr. Foster, I'm sorry to have to be the one to tell you this, but your wife was killed during a bombing in Battle Mountain three nights ago."

Foster's skin paled, his mouth parting on a strong

exhale. In a flash of a moment, the single father had gone from panicked suspect to sufficiently grieving actor. He seemed to realize he had yet to respond and turned to set the toddler in a nearby pack-and-play. Threading his hands through unkempt hair, Foster fisted two chunks and pulled. "I don't understand. You're saying she's dead? What…what was she doing in Battle Mountain?"

"That's what we're here to find out." Cree cut his attention to Alma, and her pulse ticked higher, before he turned expectantly to Sergeant Hale.

"Travis, I need you to go over what happened in the days leading up to Erica's disappearance again." Hale ducked his chin, his voice softening. "I know we've been through it before when you filed the missing person report, but now that we know what happened to her, it'll help figure out who could've done this."

A line of tears welled in the suspect's eyes, right on time. Foster released the hold on his hair and glanced down at his son. "I knew something bad had happened. I knew she wouldn't have left us if she didn't have a choice." He turned the fire building in his gaze onto Sergeant Hale. "I told you something was wrong, but you said there wasn't anything you could do. You tried to convince me she ran because of some pressure to be a good mom." Foster stretched one hand out and knocked a stack of baby books off the top of the television. The books slammed against the far wall or fell short, and battle-ready tension instantly tightened the muscles down Alma's spine. The toddler whimpered from his pack-and-play. "She loved Ethan. She never would've left him—she never would've left me—unless she had to, and now she's dead!"

Cree stepped forward, almost putting himself between her and their prime suspect, and she tugged the Taser in her belt free, but Sergeant Hale motioned for her to wait. She hadn't been an officer long, but there'd been plenty of times she'd read about domestic calls going wrong. She wouldn't let Cree become a statistic. He kept his distance, raising his palms out. "Mr. Foster, I understand what you're feeling right now. You're hurt, you're angry, you're grieving and in shock. It's an unpredictable cocktail you're not sure how to process, but I need you to remember your son is here. I know for a fact you love him. I saw it in the way you held him, how you unconsciously ran your fingers through his hair. He needs you to stay calm so no one else gets hurt. Okay? Can you do that?"

The tension intensified as Alma tried to predict the suspect's behavior. Cree wasn't on active duty anymore, but he'd stepped up to neutralize the situation all the same. He'd taken control, and the part of her she'd tried to forget, the part that had led her to becoming a Battle Mountain police officer in the first place, appreciated the effort. She had no objectivity here. The questions about restraining orders, the paranoia Hale described, the sudden disappearance of their victim—all of it had the potential to fit domestic abuse. Not to mention Travis Foster owned a construction company where the C4 used in the bomb could've originated.

"She wouldn't have left us," Foster said.

Soft sobs filled the small living room as the toddler took in every second, every movement. Foster's shoulders shook under the emotional weight, and Alma set her thumb to the side of the Taser's trigger. The worst of the storm was passing, but she'd let her guard down one too many times before. Alma licked suddenly dry lips and reached into her pants pocket. She holstered the Taser, then slowly unpocketed the shiny white gold locket and held it out, and Sergeant Hale relaxed in her peripheral vision. "Mr. Foster, do you recognize this?"

Dark eyes locked onto the trinket and widened. Shock carved deep lines in Foster's forehead as he closed the distance between them. Cree maneuvered to intercept, but Alma shook her head. Weathered hands—working hands—handled the delicate chain with respect, but Foster didn't move to take the locket from her. "Where did you get this?"

"The night of the bombing, I responded to a suspicious activity call. As I was searching the area, I found this. A few seconds later, I found your wife." An invisible blaze of rage charged up her throat, and Alma set the locket in Foster's hand. "It's Erica's, isn't it?"

He pried open the latch, letting her keep hold of the chain. A watery smile eased the shock from his expression as he studied the photo of his child secured inside. "The locket was meant to be an engagement present. We were going to get married, finally. She never took it off. Never." Inspecting the chain, he seemed on the verge of collapse and raised his gaze to hers. "Please tell me who did this to my wife."

"We're still trying to find that out. You should know I spoke to her, Mr. Foster." She studied the slightest changes in the suspect's expression, body language, weight distribution—anything to give her confirmation of what her gut was telling her was true. Acid burned up her throat as Foster's gaze leveled with hers, and the urge to rip the locket from his hand increased. She couldn't let something so precious to their victim to be left in the hands of the man who'd most likely killed her. "Did you know she was still alive when you attached the bomb to her stomach? Did you know the last thing she did was save my life by telling me to run before the explosion ripped her apart?"

"What?" Travis took a step back.

"Officer Majors, you are sorely out of line here." Sergeant Hale stepped into her peripheral vision, a warning. Cree held one arm out to stop his approach.

"What are you talking about?" Foster's attention

racquetballed between her and Hale. The mask of the grieving husband disintegrated in the blink of an eye and exposed the lying bastard beneath as he pulled back his shoulders. "That's why you're here? To accuse me of killing my wife? I never would've hurt Erica. I loved her. I have since I was sixteen years old. We have a child together, for crying out loud."

Cree brushed his arm against hers, but the contact didn't hold the same reaction as before. Where he'd settled the nervousness eating her from the inside a few moments ago, now there was only annoyance. Adrenaline spiked in her veins, and her heart rate rocketed. One in four women experienced domestic violence from their partner, and he was just going to pretend the signs weren't there? "Alma, let's get some fresh air."

"No." She shoved away from him. "I know you killed Erica, Travis. I know you're the one who strapped your wife with that bomb to destroy the evidence and any chance of us identifying her, but it didn't work. You left that note on my door after breaking into my apartment to warn me to back off, but I'm not going to stop. You're not going to get away with this."

Foster turned toward Sergeant Hale. "Are you just going to stand there and let her accuse me of killing Erica, or are you going to do your damn job?" He faced off with Alma and pointed toward the front door. "Get the hell out of my house. All of you."

"Come on." Cree threaded his hand between her ribs and arm and maneuvered her toward the front door, but she wasn't going to turn her back on a man suspected of hurting his wife. Not again.

Faster than she expected, a flood of cool air worked beneath her collar and along the back of her neck, but it failed to appease her fight-or-flight instincts. The front door slammed behind them, and it was only then she realized Sergeant Hale had stayed inside. Alma wrenched away from her partner and marched across the driveway, the locket still in hand. Every cell in her body needed distance between them, but she refused to run from her problems. Not after what she'd survived. "What the hell was that? You could've backed me up in there. He did it, Cree. Foster killed his wife, and he thinks he's going to get away with it."

"That might be the case, but we can't charge him with anything without evidence. You know that." Cree approached with caution. A combination of concern and exasperation etched into his expression and stole some of the heat from her anger. He reached for her, softly latching onto her upper arms. "You're tired, you're running on empty and you're on edge from everything that's happened the past few days. With damn good reason. Let's get back to Battle Mountain and touch base with your chief. The Silverton bomb squad might've found something we can use. Okay?"

She nodded as the anger she'd relied on to get her through the last few minutes of the interview dissipated. He was right. They didn't have enough evidence on Foster to make an arrest, but that didn't lessen her confidence Foster had been involved in his wife's death. Alma studied the front window of the town house before Cree directed her toward his pickup, recalling the computer disassembled in the living room.

Their suspect stared out at them from the other side, his toddler back on his hip, then Foster closed the curtain.

CREE HAULED THE comforter toward the ceiling and centered it across the bed.

Coming back to Battle Mountain should've brought a sense of relief, but the return trip had drained him dry. Alma hadn't said a word, only staring out the window for the entire two hours. Hell, he'd made a mess of things between them. Any progress he'd achieved in getting his partner to open up had been shattered the moment he hadn't backed her up during Travis Foster's interview.

The bathroom door clicked open, and Alma emerged clinging to her uniform, holster complete with gun and her boots to her chest. Tendrils of wet hair cascaded over the too big T-shirt he'd lent her and soaked through to her skin. The effect exaggerated the fatigue etched into her face, but the fact she was still standing after everything testified to the strength she'd developed the past few years.

"I've almost got the bed ready." Cree smoothed the lumps from the comforter with a few pointed slides of his hand, but there wasn't anything he could do in this room to make it feel less barren or more welcoming. He didn't know how to do…this. Taking others into consideration hadn't been a big focus while his grandfather was teaching him to survive in the middle of nowhere. His parents had never shown him any—still didn't—and for the first time since he'd walked away from his career, he wasn't sure how to proceed. He rubbed his hands together, a distraction from studying the long length of her legs partially hidden under the pair of boxers he'd lent her. "How…how are you feeling?"

"Better. Thank you. I think the smoke smell in my hair is finally starting to wash out." Alma scanned the space he'd claimed as his bedroom the past eight months, and embarrassment turned his insides. "I, um, wanted to talk to you about earlier."

"Okay." He straightened, mentally preparing for another assault.

"You were right about Travis Foster. We don't have enough evidence for me to make the kind of accusation I did, and I'm sorry I yelled at you for not backing me up." She smoothed her thumb over the shiny Battle Mountain Police Department badge still pinned to her uniform as though it gave her a bit of comfort. "You were just doing your job. I obviously wasn't thinking very clearly in the moment, and I let my own experiences color the situation. It won't happen again."

Cree swallowed the thickness building in his throat as his own past crept into the cracks of this investigation. He'd left the bomb squad behind, but the memories were still there. The failures, the wins, the screams and the praises—there was no running from it. No changing it. "Yes, it will."

Shock chased back the exhaustion darkening the circles under her eyes, and she clutched her uniform tighter. "If you don't think I'm fit for duty—"

"Alma." He rounded the end of the bed and reached for the mass of fabric and steel she insisted using as a protective barrier between them. Taking her uniform and weapon, he set them on the end of the bed. "Everything you've been through, all the pain, the nightmares and raw sensitivity and awareness—it's part of you now. It's what molded you into the woman standing in front of me, and as much as you want to ignore it or make it so it doesn't affect you, that's never going to happen. It's going to influence your decision-making on the job. It's going to make you question yourself twice. But ultimately, it's what's going to save the next woman in the same position you were in, and that is something you don't ever have to apologize for."

Her bottom lip parted a split second before Alma

crushed her mouth to his. Stirring heat rushed under his skin as she pressed herself against him. His hands dropped to her waist, doing everything in their power to bring her closer. Lean muscle flexed and released under his palms, and the entire world threatened to tip on its axis. Mint toothpaste exploded across his tongue as she broke through the seam of his lips, and in that moment, he was lost. It didn't matter that they were partners, that having her stay in his apartment for the night was completely unprofessional or that once this case was solved they'd go their separate ways. He wanted her. Not just the pieces she'd let him see. He wanted it all. Every ounce. Every inch. Everything, and he wanted to give her every part of himself in return.

Three hard knocks at the front door pulled him back from the brink. Disorientation overwhelmed his control as he noted the flush in her face. He worked to contain his own physiological reaction and forced himself to release her. There were only two people who'd known Alma would be staying the night. Chief Ford and his counterpart, Easton. The only reason they'd make contact was because of the case. "I think that's probably for you."

"Unless Mrs. Faris is here for a date you forgot to reschedule." She brushed her fingertips across her lips, hiding a brief smile. The same desire that had pulled him beneath the surface swam in her eyes.

"I'll just… Yeah." Alma turned on her bare heels and strode down the hallway straight to the front door.

He made quick work of replaying the kiss they'd shared in his head as he straightened her uniform on the bed. He'd give her some privacy. Because, honestly, he didn't want to know BMPD's next steps in the case. He and Alma had done their job. They'd identified the victim left at the bottom of the gulch, and the logical part of him understood that landmark in the investigation concluded their partnership. Whatever the chief or Easton had to say, he was happy to stay in ignorance. At least for a little while longer.

What had started as a duty to ensure no one was hurt during the bombing had quickly turned into something more. Because of Alma. She'd burned through his determination to detach from the past and showed him there was life after pain, that no matter what happened, he was still here. He could still do good, and hell, if he didn't want more of that in his life. More of her. Not only had she trusted him to work this case beside her but she'd relied on him. Made him feel capable, confident, useful. Strong, even, and he didn't want to let that go.

"Everything okay out there?" Cree brushed his cracked fingertips over the gold shield pinned to the breast of her uniform. No answer. He moved in line with the bedroom door standing wide open. Confusion rippled down his spine as a sweet summer breeze filled the apartment. "Alma?"

He could've sworn he'd heard her say something when she opened the door, but Cree didn't hear anything now. His fingers tingled, and he curled them into fists at his sides. Alma wouldn't have just left without telling him, especially not dressed in an extra set of his pajamas. Cree scanned the small bathroom off to his right. No movement. Nothing to suggest she was even still in the apartment. The kitchen was just as empty, and he moved into the front living room. Something wasn't right. "Are you here?"

A small piece of paper tumbled end over end before catching on the carpet past the entryway. Cree stomped on one side before it had the chance to escape. He read the handwritten scroll on one side, an exact match to the handwriting from the note left on Alma's apartment door. *You should've listened.*

Cree shoved the note in his pocket and launched out the front door. Shadows crawled up the walls of the corridor between their apartments, the outline of crime scene tape still visible across Alma's door. The bomber had known. The SOB had anticipated she'd stay in Cree's apartment and come for her when he'd least expected it.

Leaves shook under the stress of the wind in both directions and blocked any sounds that would give him an idea of which direction the bastard had taken her. Damn it. He headed for the nearest staircase, almost tripping over his own feet as he hit the landing. They couldn't have gotten far. He could still find her. He had to find her. "Alma!"

No response.

He sprinted toward his truck, digging his keys from his jeans, and wrenched open the driver's-side door. It wasn't a coincidence they'd uncovered the victim's identity only to have Alma vanish into thin air twelve hours later. He should've been on guard. He should've protected her better. His heart pounded too hard behind his ears as he shoved the key into the ignition and twisted.

The engine clicked but refused to turn over.

He tried again and pumped the accelerator. Adrenaline kept his body fine-tuned to external threats, and after the second try to start the engine logic crept in. His brain caught up. Too late. "Oh, hell."

Cree shouldered out of the truck.

Fire burned down his back and thrust him across the parking lot. He slammed into a vehicle two stalls over—Mr. Heinz's rusted Cadillac—as the explosion tore across the asphalt. Pain ricocheted around his head and down his legs, too familiar. Debris shot in every direction. The dragon raged to life as it fed off the gasoline in the truck's reservoir. His skin blistered from proximity, and Cree collapsed to the pavement.

Darkness encroached around the edges of his vision, but he couldn't stop. He couldn't stay here without putting his own life at risk. Black smoke tendrilled up into the cloudless night as distinctive shouts filled his ears. In seconds, the distant wail of a siren countered the pop and crack of the flames. Every muscle in his body begged for relief as Cree pulled himself over the curb and across the sidewalk. Warm grass worked to catch him but only managed to aggravate the burns along his arms and neck. "Alma."

Eruptions of memory contorted right in front of him as the past weaved into the present. The sirens, the groans of pain, thick smoke drilling into his lungs, the carnage—he couldn't escape. Inky spiderwebs closed in and numbed the burn of pain down his back and arms, but it wouldn't be enough to counter the guilt clawing to the surface.

He'd failed all over again.

Chapter Eight

"How long did you expect me to fall for your little charade, Officer Majors?"

Pain lanced through the side of her head and down into her injured shoulder as Alma struggled to right herself. Her wrists refused to support her upper body as she shoved against wet earth. Instead, her shoulder sunk deeper into the marshland and threatened to give way completely as she tried to bring her hands forward. The last seconds of consciousness seeped back into her memory. The knock at Cree's front door, the feel of hot summer heat spreading across her legs as she answered. Confusion when no one had been on the other side. Then agony as something fast and hot had pinched the side of her neck.

Humidity climbed deep into her lungs as she shifted her weight into her hips. The clothing Cree had lent her had soaked through. The question hanging between her and her abductor solidified as the fog cleared. Alma set her head against something spongey and closed her eyes to catalog her surroundings. Moss? "As long as it took."

Mud suctioned under the weight of heavy footsteps nearby, but her vision hadn't adjusted to the darkness yet. Before she had a chance to gauge her abductor's location, a dark outline centered above her. "You should've left well enough alone."

The voice warbled from the low ringing in her ears. But not enough to convince Alma the killer standing over her fit the original profile. According to Cree, most bombings were committed by males, but the distinct curves against the backdrop of millions of stars above suggested Erica Harmon had been murdered by a woman. Alma breathed through the damp muck permeating every fiber of her clothing and hair, but nothing discharged the savage pain in her side. "Let me guess. Because now you're going to kill me?"

"You catch on quick." The killer retreated from Alma's limited vision. "Hope you don't mind, but I removed your shoulder sling and jewelry. Can't have anyone identifying your remains before I'm ready."

"Like we did with Erica's locket. That's why you were in my apartment, wasn't it? You wanted it back." A ring of trees pulled away from the velvet of the night. She tested the plastic biting into the hypersensitized skin of her ankles. She couldn't have been unconscious long without the use of a sedative, which meant her abductor couldn't have taken her far from

Battle Mountain. A few miles at most. Small details defined themselves around her as her senses caught up to adjust to her situation. Trees. Moss. Mud. The ringing in her ears subsided as she held her breath. Water lapped a few feet behind her, and Alma gritted her teeth as rocks cut into her side from the slightest shift of her weight. Not Gunnison River. Too calm. The only other body of water near town was the lake. "San Cristobal," she whispered to herself.

It would be easy enough for the bomber to dispose of her remains in a place like this. Days, months, years would go by without so much as a shard of bone to identify.

"She fought back much harder than I expected. After I'd stabbed her, she tossed the locket so I wouldn't be able to find it. Told me I'd never know what it felt like to love anyone other than myself. I couldn't waste time trying to find it in that garbage heap, but the good news is I learn from my mistakes." A punctured click of metal pierced through the hard thud of Alma's pulse behind her ears. Another squelch of mud hiked her heart rate into overdrive a split second before the shadow of Erica Harmon's killer solidified. "You're much smarter than I gave you credit for. It's too bad. I think you could've made a real difference with your new career, but you know as well as I do I can't have you getting in my way again. I mean, did you really think I wouldn't be watching the investigation into the bombing?"

The moonless night failed to highlight any of the woman's identifying features, but the low, whiskey-smooth voice etched itself into Alma's brain. She'd never forget that voice. The calmness, the confidence, the slight upturn of pitch on the victim's name. "You killed her. Erica."

A humorless laugh filtered through the slight uptick of panic infusing along Alma's spine. "Seems my plan to destroy every piece of her in that gulch worked. You and your department—your partner from Larimer County—you don't even know who you're investigating, but I guess it doesn't matter now. Your forensic lab might be able to run DNA on the bone you recovered, but they won't have anything to compare it to. She was too careful. Managed to hide from me for the better part of a decade, but she made a mistake. She fell in love. Had a baby. You wouldn't imagine how easy it was to find her after that."

A rip of Velcro raised the hairs on the back of her neck, and Alma pressed her heels into the soggy mud holding her hostage. The bomber had done her due diligence. She'd studied the investigating officers on the case. She'd planned for every variable, and the location she'd chosen for her victims would guarantee a win. The stink of marshland soaked into Alma's pores. With the lake behind her and miles of wilderness on the other three sides, she'd never stand a chance, but she had to try. A hard edge of weight pressed into her gut and emptied her lungs. "Why?"

"Why?" the bomber asked. "Do you know how it feels to be outshone in every way? To be told to be more like someone else, that you're not good enough the way you are? No matter how hard you try, they're always going to be better. At baking, at family game night, at manners. They're always going to get the first serving of dessert and get to sit in the front seat of the car next to your parents. They're always going to be the favorite, and you…you're always going to disappoint. No matter how hard you try to prove otherwise. No matter how you try to change, they don't love you the same."

Dryness charged down Alma's throat as her ex-husband's verbal assaults superimposed over the killer's voice. There had been times in her marriage she'd believed him, that she'd felt bad for her success because it pained him so deeply. That she was the worthless one. That she was the reason for his unhappiness. Blindsided by that hurt, Alma curled two fingers into her palms just as Easton had taught her during their stint together in the rehab facility he'd founded on his family's land. The organization hadn't just been for soldiers suffering from PTSD like him or for his fiancée trying to relearn how to walk, but for anyone who'd needed support. Physically. Emotionally. The therapists there had taught her one mantra to get her through the flashbacks:

stay in the moment. She pressed her short fingernails into the tender skin of her palms and counted
off her pulse. One. Two. Three. Four. Five. Her forced
breathing ripped her from one impossible situation
into the most recent. Warm liquid bubbled from her
palms, but the pain of drawing blood would center
her. "You knew her. The woman you killed."

"My sister deserved every ounce of pain she suffered." The killer's voice dipped an octave as she
secured something to Alma's midsection. "It didn't
matter I exceeded their expectations and actually
made something of myself while she decided to
dance through life. She turned our parents against
me. They applauded her for her creativity while my
choice to investigate explosives and arson cases was
ignored at every family dinner, every holiday. They
wanted to know about my sister's rehearsals, the cos-
tumes, the locations, the other dancers and if she'd
injured herself." Another bitter laugh rippled into
the night. "Not one of them visited me in the hospital after I'd been shot on an undercover assignment gone wrong, Not once had anyone ever asked
me about my work. Not once did they decide I was
worth the effort."

A low, electrical buzz filled Alma's ears, and understanding hit. A bomb. The killer was going to
stick with her MO to make Alma disappear. She
had one chance to make it out of this alive and let
Chief Ford, Easton and Cree know where she was.

It all depended on her next move. Alma pressed her shoulders into the soft earth. The mud would make escape difficult, but she didn't have any shoes to worry about slowing her down. "You're a bomb squad tech."

"No, Officer Majors. I'm not, but if you can believe it, I've actually met Cree Gregson once before. I've been doing this job for so long that I can assemble a device with my eyes closed, which, as it turns out, is a nice skill when you're committing murder in the middle of nowhere." A flicker of red LED lights exploded from Alma's side. The square designs quickly rearranged themselves into a readable countdown. One minute. Long, gloved fingers moved a coiled wire from the front of the device to the back. The light-colored outline of C4 molded into bricks separated from the encroaching darkness.

Alma tried to sit up, but the killer slammed her back to the ground with the force of one foot. The countdown illuminated a lean frame and long dark hair but not much else. No identifying marks. Nothing Alma could use after she escaped. Because she would escape.

"Tsk, tsk, tsk. Now you're not going to make me stab you like I had to stab my sister, are you, Officer Majors?" The bomber reached behind her. The glint of metal in the red lighting reflected back into Alma's eyes. "Believe me. None of this is personal, and I wouldn't want to make you suffer any more than you have to."

"Don't worry about me. I can take care of myself." Alma rolled out from beneath the killer's boot. Rocks pierced through the soft muscle of her arms and hips as she rolled. Twice. Three times. Agony ripped through her middle with every jar of the device strapped to her front, but she wouldn't stop. No matter how long it took to escape. No matter how far she had to run. Dizziness threatened to steal her control as she brought her zip-tied hands down and tucked her knees into her chest. The edge of the tie around her wrists caught on her heel and slowed her down, but while her abductor could assemble a bomb with her eyes closed, she couldn't follow Alma in the dark. Not after she lost the neon billboard displaying her position. She crouched hard and fast to break the ties around her ankles but collapsed to one knee as the pain in her side raged. The tie had broken, and it was only a hard swing of her arms that severed the one around her wrists. She pressed her hand over the bomb, searching for the strap securing it to her midsection.

"You're going to want to keep your eye on that clock, Officer Majors." The killer's outline dissipated into a wall of trees. A flashlight beam cut through the night from the bomber's position a split second before she tossed it toward Alma. The flashlight thudded hard against the ground.

The beam lit a soft halo around Alma's feet. She ducked her chin to read the monitor. The countdown had already begun. She didn't know anything about disarming the device. She had less than forty seconds to get as far from the blast as possible. She traced the edges of the device with both hands but failed to find a strap. It was then she noted the dark color spreading across Cree's white T-shirt from beneath the device.

Twenty seconds.

Air crushed from her lungs. Mud, even watered down, didn't spread like that. Which meant… Blood.

"No. No, no, no, no." The killer had threaded the line through the C4 and sewn it directly to Alma's torso. She gripped one end of the device and pulled. Lightning struck from the edges of her vision and charged across her midsection.

Ten seconds.

She'd escaped her abusive, narcissistic ex and survived. This wasn't how she was going to die. Not when the future had finally started looking so bright.

Five seconds.

Alma closed her eyes. She was out of time.

CREE KEPT HIS distance as fire crews extinguished the last of the blaze.

Stinging pain burned down his neck and face as the same EMT who'd seen to Alma assessed his wounds. The ointment helped, but there wasn't much else they could do for this kind of injury in the field. He'd learned from experience.

Red and blue patrol lights cut across his vision as Easton Ford shoved from the passenger side of the vehicle short of stopping. Guarded concern etched deep into his expression as he rounded the hood and stalked toward Cree. "What the hell happened, Gregson?" Easton fisted each side of Cree's jacket and shoved him against the back door of the ambulance. The former Green Beret had a reputation for a short fuse and a protective streak, especially for the women in his life. "Alma was supposed to be safe with you, damn it. You knew the bastard was targeting her, and you let her out of your sight."

"I told you everything I remember on the phone." Cree pushed back, aggravating the burns along his arms, but he couldn't fault the deputy for his misdirected anger. Hell, if anything he deserved worse. "One minute she was there, the next she was gone. I didn't see a damn thing before it was too late."

Chief Ford ripped his brother back. "Go get witness statements from the neighbors. It's possible one of them saw which direction Alma was taken. That's an order." He didn't wait for an answer. The chief directed his attention to the EMT. "Any casualties?"

"No, sir. Mr. Gregson sustained the worst of it," the EMT said.

"Good. Be somewhere else, then." Battle Mountain's first line of defense settled that unreadable gaze on Cree as the EMT gave them space. "I'm not here to issue fault, Gregson. I just need to know where my officer is. You and I both know Officer Majors is more than capable of protecting herself, but this killer is determined to hide their tracks. They've already killed one victim, attempted three more and blown up your truck for good measure. I've dealt with serial killers before, but bombers are your territory. Who the hell are we looking for and what do they want with Alma?"

Cree couldn't breathe, couldn't think. Old wounds itched with remembered pain across his shoulders and down his back, but he couldn't let the past threaten the present. Not with Alma out there. "I'm not a profiler. All I can tell you is whoever is behind this knows what they're doing. Wiring a bomb to detonate when a vehicle's engine starts is more complicated than putting together a few components from an electronics store and a set of instructions off the internet." Heat intensified the sting along his neck and face as he studied the flames. He pointed to what was left of his truck. "Think about what we have so far. The person who killed Erica Harmon didn't want to risk leaving behind evidence to identify her. That tells me this is someone who's studied forensics." He ticked off his index finger then moved onto the middle. "The bomber knew we'd trace the components of the initial explosion back to Galaxy Electronics, beat us to it and got rid of any video evidence they'd been there. That tells me they've worked investigations." He pressed his sore palm into his ring finger. "And the fact they know how to not only build a device but wire a vehicle to explode upon ignition… That tells me they were professionally trained."

Chief Ford straightened and stood a bit taller. The last of the flames sizzled under the onslaught of the fire hose and targeted attacks from the fire crew, kicking up steam behind him. "That doesn't sound like a civilian with a grudge against the victim. You're talking about an investigator."

"Yeah, I am." The pieces lined up, creating a blurry puzzle he couldn't see yet, but for the time being, it was his leading theory.

The chief removed his ten-gallon hat and pushed his hair back off his forehead. The patrol car's lights reflected off the large belt buckle at his waist and burned Cree's retinas. "Hell. I've got an APB out for Officer Majors and put Macie on the phones. If we're looking for a trained explosives investigator, it stands to reason they're being careful. Avoiding main roads and nosy neighbors. Somewhere out of town—"

A secondary explosion had Cree and the rest of the first responders ducking toward the ground. He twisted around and caught sight of a high plume of fire to the west. The nerve endings that hadn't been burned by the inferno of his truck turned to ice. "Alma." Cree scanned the parking lot as gut-wrench-

FREE BOOKS GIVEAWAY

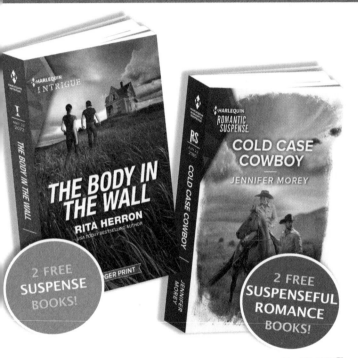

YOU pick your books – WE pay for everything.

You get up to FOUR New Books and TWO Mystery Gifts...absolutely FREE!

Dear Reader,

I am writing to announce the launch of a huge **FREE BOOKS GIVEAWAY**... and to let you know that YOU are entitled to choose up to FOUR fantastic books that WE pay for.

Try **Harlequin® Romantic Suspense** books featuring heart-racing page-turners with unexpected plot twists and irresistible chemistry that will keep you guessing to the very end.

Try **Harlequin Intrigue® Larger-Print** books featuring action-packed stories that will keep you on the edge of your seat. Solve the crime and deliver justice at all costs.

Or TRY BOTH!

In return, we ask just one favor: Would you please participate in our brief Reader Survey? We'd love to hear from you.

This FREE BOOKS GIVEAWAY means that your introductory shipment is completely free, even the shipping! If you decide to continue, you can look forward to curated monthly shipments of brand-new books from your selected series, always at a discount off the cover price! Plus you can cancel any time. Who could pass up a deal like that?

Sincerely

Pam Powers

Pam Powers
For Harlequin Reader Service

Complete the survey below and return it today to receive up to 4 FREE BOOKS and FREE GIFTS guaranteed!

FREE BOOKS GIVEAWAY
Reader Survey

1

Do you prefer stories with suspenful storylines?

◯ YES ◯ NO

2

Do you share your favorite books with friends?

◯ YES ◯ NO

3

Do you often choose to read instead of watching TV?

◯ YES ◯ NO

YES! Please send me my Free Rewards, consisting of **2 Free Books** from each series I select and **Free Mystery Gifts**. I understand that I am under no obligation to buy anything, no purchase necessary see terms and conditions for details.

❏ Harlequin® Romantic Suspense (240/340 HDL GRRU)
❏ Harlequin Intrigue® Larger-Print (199/399 HDL GRRU)
❏ Try Both (240/340 & 199/399 HDL GRR6)

FIRST NAME

LAST NAME

ADDRESS

APT.#

CITY

STATE/PROV.

ZIP/POSTAL CODE

EMAIL ❏ Please check this box if you would like to receive newsletters and promotional emails from Harlequin Enterprises ULC and its affiliates. You can unsubscribe anytime.

HI/HRS-122-FBG22

ing nausea churned. He closed the distance between him and the chief and stretched out his hand. "I need your keys."

"That's my officer. I'm driving." Chief Ford issued an ear-splitting whistle of several notes as he rounded the hood and wrenched open the driver's-side door.

Cree collapsed into the passenger seat and slammed the door behind him. He spotted Easton Ford skipping the last few stairs of the apartment complex and sprinting toward the car. He clenched the dashboard to counter the unbalance wrecking through him at the thought of Alma caught in the latest explosion. "Did you seriously just whistle for your brother to heel?"

"Works every time." Chief Ford threw the patrol car into Reverse and stepped on the accelerator. He whipped the back end into the lot, barely missing the ambulance with the hood, and slammed on the brakes. Easton threw the back door open and climbed inside a split second before the screech of tires filled the small cabin of the vehicle. "Those flames are coming from outside town. Near the lake."

The map Cree had memorized as a teen growing up with his grandfather on the outskirts of town filtered through his mind. It had been years since he'd paid a visit. So much had already changed, and he couldn't rely on his history to comfort the anxiety clawing up his throat. "What's out there?"

"Nothing much. A few hunting cabins that only get used a few months out of the year. Mostly marshland." Chief Ford took a hard right turn onto Highway 149, and momentum shifted Cree to the other side of the car. The chief detached the radio strapped to the dashboard and hit the push-to-talk button. "Dispatch, I need fire and rescue redirected out to San Cristobal Lake ASAP. We've got another explosion, and I don't want to take the chance of those flames spreading."

"You got it, Chief," Macie said.

The weight of Weston Ford's quick assessment lodged air in Cree's throat while pressure built between his shoulder blades thanks to the man's brother in the back seat. He could practically feel their concern and anxiety when it came to Alma. "Alma is a good officer. She knows what she's doing."

"I hope you're right." Cree gripped the handle above his head tighter than necessary, but it was the only thing keeping him grounded as seconds distorted into minutes and then into what felt like an hour. Town limits bled to flat valleys and mountainous peaks. The trees grew thicker and the darkness heavier.

Until an orange glow up ahead consumed their attention.

Cree pressed his heels into the floor as he took in the expanse of flames spreading fast.

"Holy hell." Easton threaded all ten fingers

through the metal web barricading the back seat from the front.

The chief got back on the radio as heat penetrated through the windows and the vehicle's frame. "Dispatch, this fire is eating through everything in its path. Get Silverton and Ouray fire and rescue out here and issue an evacuation order now!"

Macie's voice barely pierced through the hard thud of Cree's pulse at the base of his skull. Chief Ford brought the vehicle to a complete stop, and Cree hit the dirt. He jogged toward the first wall of flames as they licked up pines and devoured the brush across the wilderness floor.

"Gregson, you can't go in there!" Easton's voice penetrated through the roar and pop of the fire as a strong grip wrapped around his arm. "You won't make it a dozen feet before that fire eats you alive. You need to wait for fire and rescue!"

"I'm not leaving her!" Cree shoved the former soldier off. Sweat built along the sides of his face and pooled under his collar. The burns along his neck protested every second he held firm. He was the reason Alma had been taken in the first place. He wasn't going to fail her now. Peeling his jacket from his shoulders, he ducked beneath the fabric. "I need water."

Easton Ford rounded back into the patrol car and popped the trunk. Grabbing three water bottles, he handed off two to Cree and soaked his own jacket with the third.

"What are you doing?" Cree asked.

"You're not the only one who cares about what happens to Alma. We'll find her faster if we split up." Easton accepted the handheld radio his brother offered and clipped it to his belt, Cree doing the same. "Where did the fire originate?"

Cree scanned the fiery landscape. Every second they wasted with logistics was another second Alma didn't have, but they couldn't search this entire area blind, either. He pointed to the collection of trees and bushes at an angle. The blast from the explosive had knocked them off center. Water dripped from the hem of his jacket as he set it over his head and shoulders. "There. About one hundred yards northeast."

"You search there. I'll take the perimeter in case she got away," Easton said.

"I'll give you five minutes! Stay in radio contact. If it gets to be too much, back out." Chief Ford nodded to Gregson and slapped his brother on the back. He raised his voice over the roar of the draft. "Fire and rescue is on the way."

Cree dashed for the epicenter of the flames, his vision too narrow with the addition of the jacket on his head, but he couldn't risk not having the extra protection. The hairs on his forearm singed as the blaze closed in. He jumped over the downed tree just as the flames cut him off from Easton and Chief Ford.

Heat burned down his throat. It was getting harder to breathe, but he wouldn't stop. Not until he found her.

"Alma!" Trees hissed and popped in response. Charred earth spread out in front of him, but there was no sign of her. She was out here. She was alive. He had to believe that. He wasn't sure how much time had passed. Didn't care about Ford's five-minute deadline. He was going to find her. The fire raged as though feeding off the desperation boiling over inside. He lifted the protection from his head and flinched from the intensity. Wavering flames reflected back to him from the lake. "Alma!"

Coughing reached his ears from the left. "Cree?"

Every cell in his body homed on his name. The last of his adrenaline burned off in his veins as he stepped over a grouping of devastated twigs and brush. He'd heard her. It wasn't his mind playing tricks on him. "Tell me where you are!"

"Here." Another round of coughing broke through the howl of the inferno. Then he saw movement. A hand stretched toward him through the surface of the murky water, and Cree lost his protection to reach her faster.

"Alma." He hauled himself through the marsh and swam out to meet her. The soles of his shoes failed against the algae rocks, and he went down. Soaked head to foot, Cree pulled her against his chest as the fire raged around them. "I've got you."

Chapter Nine

She'd run out of time.

Alma rolled her face away from the itchy hospital bed pillows and scanned one side of the room. The medical center in the middle of town wasn't much with its dated equipment and small patient rooms, but what it lacked for in modernity it more than paid off in staff. The emergency room physician had stopped the bleeding in her side, but it would take time and skin grafts to put her back together fully. The scent of antiseptic and sweat filled her lungs...with a hint of smoke. The reminder should've scared her, but there was only one reason her room would smell like that. "Didn't they make you change your clothes when you got here?"

A deep rumble of a laugh chased back a majority of the grogginess clinging to her brain and lightened the heaviness of throwing herself back in the investigation. Where bombers killed innocent women and started forest fires. Where she was alone and didn't have anyone to fight for other than herself. "They're fresh out of scrubs, and I'm not sure the hospital staff would appreciate me walking around in my boxers."

She closed her eyes against the bright fluorescent lighting, the blood pressure cuff too tight around one arm. The monitor off to one side recorded her stats, then quickly triggered the cuff to release. Blood rushed back into her fingers as a weight in her muscles urged her into unconsciousness. Alma sank deeper into the bed. "I can lend you a blanket."

"I'll keep my clothes on, for everyone's benefit. Especially yours." Movement registered from behind, then circled around the end of her bed. A gentle weight settled on her calf, but she didn't have the inclination or the energy to pull away. In fact, the contact was nice. Solid despite his light touch, grounding.

"Prude," she said.

The slide of metal against tile urged her to open her eyes, and she found Cree pulling a chair closer to the edge of the bed. "How are you feeling?"

"Like someone sewed a bomb to my stomach and left me for dead." Fatigue lifted with every inhale, and Alma noted a red hue to his skin she could've sworn hadn't been there before. Like a sunburn. Only worse. The last few memories of panicked desperation flashed across her mind. The timer on the bomb counting down. The realization the bomber had attached the device to Alma's skin. The pain as she'd ripped the bomb free. And the suffocating sensation as she'd thrown herself into the lake. Then his voice. So clear. So close. She'd convinced herself she'd imagined it until she'd seen him fight through the flames. For her. "You're hurt."

"It's nothing I haven't survived before." He made an effort to hide the back of his free hand, but Alma threaded her fingers through the bed's guard to keep him from retreating. The course hairs she'd noted before had been burned away, exposing angry skin and burn ointment. "I only wish I'd realized you'd been taken sooner."

"That wasn't your fault. Cree, none of this was your fault." It'd been so long since she'd opened herself to the possibility of touching someone else—of being touched—that her hand shook at the contact. When was the last time she'd reached out to someone for help? When had she trusted the person on the other side wouldn't hurt her? She couldn't remember. But she trusted Cree. Not only had he walked through a physical wall of flames to get to her in time, but he'd respected her need for space when it came to their partnership. He'd saved her life, and she wasn't sure she'd ever be able to repay him for that, short of trusting him completely. But as much as she didn't want to talk about what had happened out there, they were still in the middle of a murder investigation. "Were the fire crews able to get control of the blaze?"

"They're still working on it. So far the fire has

burned around fourteen hundred acres, but the winds are pushing it into the mountains instead of into town. Your chief sent out the evacuation warning in case it changes direction. We got lucky." He smoothed cracked skin over the back of her hand, seemingly memorizing the pattern of moles and the difference in color between them. "Whoever killed Erica Harmon rigged my truck to explode when it started. They wanted me out of commission while they took you out of the investigation. If it hadn't been for Chief Ford and Easton, I wouldn't have gotten to you in time."

"Not they. She." Alma rolled her lips between her teeth and bit down to control the waver in her voice. "The bomber is a woman."

"Good to know. I know how difficult this is for you, Alma. I've been in your position. Your chief and fire and rescue want answers as to what happened out there, but I'll hold them off as long as I can if that's what you need." He brought her hand to his mouth and planted a soft kiss over the thin skin there before rubbing his own mark away. "You're recovering from surgery. If you feel that's all you can focus on right now, I'll find a way to come at this from another angle."

"I appreciate that, but no. The killer came after me. She was in my apartment to scare me. She abducted me because she knows I'm getting too close. I want to see this through to the end. I want to make sure she can't hurt anyone else." She needed to help. She needed to find the bomber before someone else ended up in Erica Harmon's position. Because if there'd been someone willing to help her when her marriage had gone to hell, she might not have suffered longer before she'd gotten the courage to claw her way out. "Has the forensic lab been able to confirm the victim's identity from the shard of bone we recovered?"

"And by recovered, you mean that time the EMT pulled it out of your shoulder? No. Not as far as I know." Confusion rippled across his forehead and deepened the lines between his eyebrows. "You identified Erica Harmon from her missing person report. Has something changed?"

The images she'd been fighting off since waking after surgery wouldn't stay buried. "I talked to her. The bomber. She told me her sister deserved every ounce of pain she suffered for ruining her life."

"We didn't find any next of kin for Erica Harmon." Cree sat a bit taller in his seat. "All we had was Travis Foster's missing person report."

"That's just it. When I was out there, she told me we didn't even know who we were investigating. Like Erica Harmon was an alias." A shudder quaked through her, and she held on to Cree's hand a bit tighter. It wasn't much, but the physical contact eased her tendency to compartmentalize and never look back. She couldn't do that here. She had to see this through. "Travis filed that report under the name Erica Harmon because that was who he knew her as before they fell in love and started a family together. He filed a second report under what would be her married name, but what if Erica lied from the beginning? What if our victim isn't who she convinced everyone she was?"

His rough exhale shook through him. "We'd be back at square one and no closer to finding who wanted her dead."

"Yeah." The monitor beeped with a warning and pulled forest green eyes to the screen. She read the concern etched into his expression before the pain burned into her awareness. Her pain medication had run low, and her side hurt worse than the time she'd dropped an archaeology trowel on her toe, but she couldn't risk letting the bomber get away again. She released her hold on Cree's hand and sucked in enough air to brace herself to sit up. And froze. Hospital staff had taken the clothes she'd borrowed from Cree into evidence. The only thing standing between them was the thin gown that didn't offer much protection in the back, and she wasn't about to take this relationship to the next level. Not yet, anyway. "We need to talk to Travis Foster again, but first I'm going to need you to turn around."

"You really think he's going to want to talk to you again?" Cree shoved to his feet, then bent at the waist to haul a duffel bag into his seat. He headed for the door, pulling up short. He wasn't going to let anyone come through that door without her permission, and she appreciated the thought more than she expected.

"I think he's going to want to hear what I have to say this time." She set her bare feet on the floor and reached for the bag. Her uniform had been cleaned and pressed, her holster, gun and badge waiting for her on top. One side of her mouth tugged higher. He'd brought her a fresh change of clothes, including a clean bra and set of underwear, knowing she wouldn't sit here while a bomber tore her town apart. Alma pulled her uniform from the bag. Ripping the blood pressure cuff from around her arm, she discarded it on the bed and slowly pulled the needle from the crook of her arm. Blood bloomed around the already-bruising area, but it was nothing compared to what she'd already survived. "If I'm right, Erica—or whoever she really is—wasn't our killer's only target."

"You're sure?" he asked.

Alma hadn't realized how many muscles in her abdomen she used for simply dressing herself each day. She sat against the bed when the pain reared its ugly head. Pressing her hand against the wound in her side, she shook her head. "It was something in her voice, the way she accused Erica of going out of her way to show up her sister by falling in love and having a kid."

"You think she might try to go after Travis and

his son." Cree's voice dropped an octave. His shoulders turned slightly toward her, but he kept his gaze boring straight into the hospital room door like the gentleman he was.

She managed to get both legs into her slacks and tugged them into place. Then her boots. After tucking her uniform shirt into her waistband as carefully as she could, Alma situated her holster, her armor back in place. "I don't know, but my gut says the grieving husband knows more than he's letting on."

HE'D NEARLY LOST HER.

Cree closed the hospital room door behind him as Alma finished getting dressed and nearly collided with two men waiting on the other side. "Chief." He nodded appreciation. "Easton."

"How's she doing?" Easton Ford angled toward the door as though prepared to check on his colleague himself but held himself back.

"She's shaken, and hell, I can't blame her. It's not every day you're abducted and wake up to find an active bomb sewn into your skin. Even in law enforcement." Cree read the concern etched into both men's expressions and tried to push as much assurance into his voice as he could. As much as he wanted to step in to be the one Alma relied on out of some sick sense of guilt, she had a lot of people who cared about her, and he wouldn't come between her and that support. "But she's strong. She's already dictating her statement into her phone so we can get back to the investigation. Anything from fire and rescue?"

"They found the device that started the blaze. Fire marshal says it's C4." Chief Ford unpocketed his phone and handed it off to Cree with a swipe of his thumb. "Looks to be the same type of device Alma saw in that gulch."

Cree scanned through the photos, detailing the shattered pieces of green motherboard and a chunk of red coiling wire. "Same components as I saw in Galaxy Electronics before it exploded, too." He handed back the phone. "At least our bomber is consistent. Alma's going to want to know how Mr. Thorp is doing since he lost the store."

"He walked away with a mild concussion. His wife's helping him through some headaches and scrapes, but he's clearheaded and asking about Alma. He wants to make sure she's doesn't feel guilty for what happened." Easton folded his arms across a broad chest honed over years of consistent discipline and training. "He isn't the only one."

Cree nodded and returned the chief's phone. The rock settling in his gut grew heavier as the events of the past three days shattered the detachment he'd kept close once he hit town. Battle Mountain was supposed to be a way station—temporary—while he summoned the courage to go back to his life. But the thought of walking away from all this, on Alma, didn't sit right. Three days. That was all it'd taken for her to pull him apart, show him what really mattered and shove all those broken pieces back together. He wasn't the same man who'd crossed the town borders eight months ago. He was stronger, more sure of himself, less isolated. He felt…almost human again. Because of her, and that wasn't something he was sure he could turn his back on once this investigation concluded. "You two know her better than I do."

"We also know she trusts you. More than she might trust either of us." Chief Ford pocketed his phone back, but the drop in the man's voice triggered Cree's defenses. "You and I both know she's not going to back off this case, even at the risk of running herself into the ground. She's got too much invested to walk away now and a hell of a lot she wants to prove. I don't know why you left Larimer County or what your plans are here in Battle Mountain, but I'm trusting you to have her back, Gregson. One officer to another. Don't let me down." The chief offered his hand.

The moment shouldn't have meant much. He'd worked this case from the beginning. He'd known exactly what he was getting into by stepping back into the field, but Cree couldn't help but let go of the shame and embarrassment that had followed him over the county line. And for the first time in months, he imagined himself taking up that shield again. Being part of something bigger, like his grandfather had always wanted. "Yes, sir."

"Silverton bomb squad's expecting us at the station. Call us if you need anything." Easton slapped him on the back and headed down the hallway, his brother on his heels. Both men rounded the corner just as the door swung open behind him.

Centering herself in the frame, Alma looked up at him with that gut-wrenching smile in place, and suddenly every cell in his body was vibrating at a higher frequency. The scrapes and bruises along one side of her face had lightened, but the sling around her arm reminded him all too quickly that she was still in danger. She leaned against the doorframe, careful of her shoulder and moving slower because of the stitches in her side. "You realize you were supposed to report back whether or not the coast was clear for me to escape, right?"

"Ran into a bit of a problem." Any other officer on the force would've taken the opportunity to recover for a few days, but none of the men or women Cree had served with had Alma's determination for justice. And damn, if that wasn't the sexiest thing he'd ever seen. "Seems you're a little too well-liked."

Her laugh filtered through a strained exhale, and Alma pressed her free hand into her side for support. Color drained from her face, but she didn't let her discomfort show, committed to seeing this through to the end. "Let me guess. Weston and Easton."

"They were worried about you." Cree banished the urge to reach for her. No matter how much he needed that physical contact to assure himself she was okay, he'd leave it to her to direct how far their relationship went. "They're not the only ones. You sure you're ready to get back out in the field?"

"You know what? I'm good. Honestly." She scanned the length of her body, still using the support of the doorframe. "It's going to take some getting used to all these stitches, but unfortunately, if I've learned anything from going through what I did with my ex-husband, it's that I've taught myself how to live in chaos and pain. I'm...comfortable there." She raised that dark gaze to his and straightened. Taking a step into him, Alma traced her thumb along his jaw. "If that changes, you'll be the first one to know. Deal?"

"Deal." He set his hand over hers, leaning into her touch. Warmth speared through the last of his reservations. Of all the things he'd expected from small-town, middle-of-nowhere living, he'd never expected her. "Ready to flee the scene?"

"It's not fleeing when I'm legally allowed to check myself out of my physician's care." She pointed toward the nurses' station and the thin man with curly dark hair dressed in a white lab coat. "All I have to do is sign the discharge papers."

"But fleeing sounds more fun, don't you think?" he asked.

A knowing smile tugged one corner of her mouth higher as she scanned the length of the corridor. The baby hairs around her temples swayed under a hit from the air conditioner above, lulling his high-strung thoughts into place. Hell, was there anything Alma couldn't do? The guarded officer he'd met the night of the first explosion took control of her expression. "All right. There are two security guards at the end of the hall. Both armed, and a network of surveillance cameras watching our every move." She motioned toward the officers with the crown of her head. "Think you can distract the guards while I make a break for it?"

"Only if you grab some of the orange Jell-O from that cart on the way out." He signaled in the opposite direction. "I'll head for the car. Rendezvous in five out the west entrance."

"Orange Jell-O? And here I thought I'd already learned about all the skeletons in your closet these past few days." Squeezing his hand, she maneuvered around him but didn't make it much farther than a couple of feet. "See you on the other side."

"With the Jell-O," he said.

"With the Jell-O." She nodded, trying to hide another smile.

Cree headed for the two guards camped out at the opposite end of the floor. Ringing phones, low conversations and announcements over the PA system kept him focused when all he wanted to do was watch Alma talk her way out of lifting orange Jell-O cups from the food cart. He waved to the officers to keep their attention on him, and not the partner he couldn't get enough of. "Hey, guys. Not sure if you know this, but I found a suspicious coin in the men's bathroom down the hall. I tried to get a closer look, but it's behind one of the urinals, and I'm just not willing to get on my hands and knees for that kind of thing. Would one of you mind taking a look for me?"

The guards looked at each other, one laughing. "A coin?"

"Yeah. I think it might be a quarter. I could really use it." Cree maneuvered around both guards to get a view of Alma, who was scrupulously checking each Jell-O color from the bottom. She stacked what looked like a collection of lime-green ones in the crook of her good arm, and the tendons in his neck tightened without permission. "Not green. I hate green." He did his best to get her attention while still appearing to be engaged in conversation with the security guards, but as Alma tossed him a smile before making her exit, the truth lay in front of him. He'd been set up. "Turns out I'm a bit of a germophobe."

"All right, buddy. Let's get you back to the psych ward on four." The smaller of the guards moved to cut off his escape, but Cree dodged the attempt.

"You know, now that I think of it, it was a button." He clicked his tongue with a strong point of his index finger while following after Alma. "Thanks for your help anyway." Jogging to catch up with her, he ignored the call of Alma's physician and a few whispered questions from visitors and nurses as he headed for the stairs. He caught sight of her long brown hair just before the door two flights down slammed shut behind her. "Now, where do you think you're going?"

Cree rushed down the stairs after her, excitement building under his skin. He exited through their agreed-upon route and hit the parking lot on the west side of the building. His lungs worked to keep up with his racing heart, but he couldn't let his guard down. Not yet. He scanned the lot and targeted the truck Easton had loaned him after they'd reached the clinic. There, leaning against the hood and peeling back the lid to a lime-green Jell-O container, stood his partner, every ounce the woman he'd started falling for. Acceptance reverberated through him. She'd won. He hiked a thumb over his shoulder as a quick laugh overwhelmed his control. Hell, it had been a long time since he'd let himself enjoy the moment. Too long. "They almost detained me."

"I would have, too," she said. "A suspicious coin?"

"I read it in an article a few years ago. The cops who responded to the call reported it was a quarter." Cree took up position against the passenger-side door as she slurped the last of her dessert. "That doesn't look orange."

She reached for the short stack of containers she'd piled on the hood of the truck, most likely slower than she would've wanted to, and tossed him one with her uninjured hand. He caught it against his chest. Orange Jell-O, the same as he'd grown up on while living off the grid with his grandfather. Alma collected the rest and moved to stand in front of him. "Thank you."

"For what?" he asked.

"Reminding me there's more to life than the chaos and pain." She rose onto her toes and pressed her mouth to his.

Chapter Ten

It was too late to haul Travis Foster into the station all the way from Ouray, and going back to her apartment wasn't an option. While the crime scene techs Chief Ford had called in to process the evidence had cleared her to move back in, she couldn't face the destruction. Not yet.

The thud of Cree's keys on the nearby table frayed her nerves. She flinched against the sensory overload as he flipped on the living room light. The pain medication from the clinic had worn thin, leaving her nerves raw and exposed. She could still distinguish his taste through the remnants of lime Jell-O at the back of her throat. A perfect combination of citrus and mint when the two shouldn't have gotten along. Their kiss had chased back the ice crystallizing in her bones and shocked her back to life in the same moment. But while she'd wanted to physically push herself to break through the chains holding her back since her divorce, other parts of her body had already started failing. He'd noticed it when she'd unwillingly swayed on her feet back in the clinic's parking lot. In what seemed like seconds, she'd gone from rebellious and playful to exhausted and beaten. Now Alma didn't know what to do, didn't know where to go from here.

"The bed is still made up. I can get you a new pair of clothes since your chief commandeered the last set as evidence." He secured the dead bolt on the front door and armed the alarm panel off to the right. Considering the last time she'd set foot in this place she'd been abducted, she imagined he wasn't willing to take any chances of her disappearing this time. "I'm not sure how much you were able to clean up at the clinic. You're welcome to take another shower if you need, and I have some leftovers in the fridge if you're hungry."

She didn't move. Couldn't. "I think I'd just like to sit down for a few minutes, if that's okay with you."

"Yeah. Sure," he said.

The tremors she'd noted in her hand on the drive back to the apartment worsened, and no amount of breath work or counting helped. Alma tried to cross her arms over her chest, but the shoulder sling stopped any attempt. The control she'd developed over this past year had started to crack, and with that realization anxiety screamed through her. Her heart rate spiked, her breath shallowing. Her body felt too light and too heavy at the same time, and nothing— not even the floor—seemed strong enough to hold her in place. She'd been through enough of these moments throughout her marriage to recognize when they got the best of her, but she'd gotten them under control. She'd risen above letting the world and everybody in it break her. "Cree, I don't seem to be able to move. Could you…"

"I've got you." Three words. The same three words he'd whispered when he'd pulled her from the lake. His strong grip grounded her as he maneuvered them toward the nearest couch. Reliable. Focused. "Sit right here. I'll get you a glass of water." His outline rounded into the kitchen, and before she had a chance to count the seconds, he was offering her a cold glass. Cree took his seat, keeping a few inches of distance between them. The couch cushion dipped under his weight, but instead of her being thrown off by the unbalance, it was reassuring having him so close. "You can be honest with me. I give you my word I won't be offended or think any less of you. Is this because of the kiss? My truck is currently a smoldering pile of metal, but I can get a hotel room for the night if you need space—"

"What? No, that's not… That's not it at all." She didn't regret the kiss, and she didn't want him to leave. Because for the first time since striking out on her own—separate from her career, her marriage, the woman she used to be—she wasn't scared. The low temperature of the glass bled into her palm and calmed her nervous system. Her humorless laugh died almost as quickly as she'd forced it free. "I guess I'm just not as unbreakable as I believed. Can't even get through one attempt on my life without having a panic attack."

Cree moved slow, slower than she wanted him to move, and set his hand on her arm. The water shook under her grip, but his hold supported her from dropping it outright. "Tell me."

"After the bombing at that conference, was there ever a moment when you told yourself that was the worst it could be? That no matter what came next, you'd survived, and you weren't going to let anything stop you from moving on?" she asked.

He removed his hand from her arm, then interlaced his fingers together between his knees. "Honestly, I tried to pretend it had never happened. I ran here, and it wasn't until recently that I even looked back." His gaze roamed over her face as though he was trying to memorize every line, every curve. Cree turned his knees into hers, his jeans brushing against her. "You? You faced your fears. You did something about it and got yourself out of an impossible situation. You're a hundred times stronger than I am for that reason alone, but I can tell from the look in your eyes you're worried you haven't recovered from what your ex-husband did."

His words settled between them, drilling straight into her core.

"I know I can't flip a switch and make everything

be okay. In my head, I know that's not how trauma works. I know there will be these times throughout my life that I'll get blindsided by something that will throw me back, but it's been a year." She struggled to take a full breath. "I feel like I should've made more progress than this, that the same things shouldn't be affecting me anymore. I left him. I got help. I moved on with my life by coming home and changing careers. What else am I supposed to do?"

"I don't know if there's anything else you can do but give it time," he said.

She curled the fingers of her uninjured hand into a fist. "I can't even stop the shaking in my hands. What if the next time my anxiety gets the best of me it's during a call? What if it happens again during this investigation?" Desperation and helplessness tornadoed through her, and she didn't know how to make it stop. "I chose to become a reserve officer so I could protect myself, but I'm not even sure I can do that anymore, let alone protect the people of this town."

"Come here." Cree secured his arms around her back and tugged her into his side. His shoulders and chest rose on exaggerated inhales, and Alma realized he was doing it for her benefit, to remind her to breathe. The physical connection was enough to anchor her in the moment, but it was his constant consideration for her well-being that drained the tension from her muscles. He settled back on the couch, bringing her along with him, as she set her ear over his heart. Calloused fingers smoothed the hair back from her face in a hypnotic rhythm as they sat there.

She wasn't sure how long. Didn't care. In the span of three days he'd done more for her than anyone she'd believed cared about her, and she never wanted to go back. To her empty apartment. To her isolated existence. To the hypersensitive paranoia that surviving had scratched into her bones. Her heart rate stabilized in a matter of minutes, and Alma took her first full breath since waking up in the hospital. "Have you thought about what you'll do after this case is closed?"

"Not really." His voice echoed through his chest and burrowed under her skin. It soothed the rough edges of her thoughts and elicited a chain reaction of desire at the same time. "I'm still with Larimer's bomb squad, but my CO told me to take as much time as I needed to get my head right. I'm on indefinite leave, and I intended to take full advantage as long as I could. But working this case with you... It's helped."

Alma pushed against him, leveling her gaze with his. Her stomach twisted as her next question formed. "You want to go back?"

"My life is there. I only came back to Battle Mountain to escape it for a while. After my discharge from the army, I made something for myself, built a career on my own. I wasn't sure I was entirely ready to let it go." He squeezed her against him. "Then Chief Ford asked me to watch your back while we were at the hospital, and I went from thinking about this case to thinking about the next one. And the one after that. There's still a lot of good I could do in Loveland. There's also a lot of good I could do here."

Apprehension coiled low in her belly as she processed his meaning one word at a time. Her voice deadpanned as all those feelings of inadequacy charged through her, and Alma untangled herself from his arms. "My CO asked you to watch my back?"

"Yeah, and I'm glad he did. Because he knows you. He knows you won't stop investigating this case, even with a torn rotator cuff and a new skin graft in your side, and Battle Mountain's department is barely functioning. The chief can only stretch himself so far, and Easton is still splitting his time between the department and the rehab center." Cree slid to the edge of the couch, setting his burned hand over hers. "This town has become the epicenter of three major cases in the past year. It doesn't have the support it needs, and neither do you."

"What are you saying?" She wouldn't let herself hope. She needed him to say it. She needed him to tell her she was worth losing the life he'd built because no one else had. "You want to transfer from Larimer County's bomb squad to a smaller department? That's career suicide."

"Yeah, it is, but there's a part of me that doesn't care." Cree framed her face with one hand and leaned in to kiss her softly. "Part of me knows partnering with you on the job and off would be worth it. You'd be worth it."

HE HAD TO get himself a new couch.

Aches and pains lightninged through his joints as Cree wrenched open the glass door of the Battle Mountain Police Station and held back to let Alma through first. The place hadn't changed since he'd been here last, but the entire world had.

Four bombings. Each designed to achieve a different goal. Murder, distraction, evidence tampering. But there was a piece of this puzzle they still couldn't see: the victim's real identity. Only Travis Foster could give them that.

He stepped over the threshold and followed his partner through the too-narrow hallways leading past the break room, the cells and the chief's office. Pressing the pads of his fingers into the tendon along his neck, Cree fought to relieve the tension that came with giving Alma the bed for the night. Then again, he'd never slept better. He was tempted to believe it was just exhaustion—maybe even his endless fantasy of what it would be like to stay in Battle Mountain—that had finally given his overactive mind a break. But Cree knew the truth. His gaze flickered to Alma as she rounded into the lobby of the station.

It was her, and once they closed this case and the paperwork cleared, he'd make it official. He wasn't going anywhere.

"Mr. Foster, I'm Chief Ford. I wanted to thank you for being here. You've already met Officer Majors and her partner, Officer Gregson." The chief came to a stop a few feet from the victim's husband, hand outstretched. Once he realized Foster wasn't going to shake, he motioned down the hall. "Why don't we talk in my office?"

"I told you people everything I knew when you came to my house and accused me of killing Erica." The circles under Foster's eyes had grown a bit darker, the hollowness Cree noted in the man's house deeper, as he took a seat in front of the chief's desk. The glare he settled on Alma raised protective instincts Cree didn't know he still had, but he would let her and the chief do their jobs without interference. "Not sure what else you want from me."

"Mr. Foster, we're very sorry for your loss." The chief removed his hat and set it off to the side, interlacing his fingers across the surface of the overrun, earth-tone-stained desk. "I've lost a spouse. I know the toll it can take on you not just in the moment but for years, and I don't wish it on anyone."

The fight left Foster's body language, and he settled deeper into his seat. "You brought me here for a reason. Have you made progress in Erica's case? Can I finally take her home?"

"Our investigation hasn't concluded." The chief nodded to Alma, who stepped forward. "I'm sure you've heard about the four bombs that have gone off here in Battle Mountain, one of which started that fire near San Cristobal Lake."

"Kind of hard to ignore." Another bout of defensiveness seemed to tense the man's shoulders as Foster pressed his heels into the industrial carpet. He bounced his gaze between the chief, then Alma and finally Cree. "You going to accuse me of setting those off, too?"

"No, sir. In fact, we have a pretty good idea of who designed and detonated the devices. We believe the initial explosion was meant to destroy any evidence of Erica's murder, and it did a damn good job," Chief Ford said. "Now, I know my deputies already questioned you about Erica when they paid a visit to your home a few days ago, but now I'm asking. Can you think of anyone who might have wanted to hurt your wife?"

Foster shook his head. "No. We were…happy."

"Sir, I owe you an apology. I was out of line when I implied you'd been the one to kill Erica, and I'm sorry." Determination laced Alma's voice, which sounded stronger than it had last night, and Cree couldn't do anything but admire her ability to keep moving forward, no matter the setback. "I realize the last thing you want to do at a time like this is answer more questions, but we need to know. Has there been anyone hanging around your home? Any calls at odd hours with no one on the other line? Issues at your construction site?"

"We had some C4 go missing from one of our projects about a month ago, but we reported it to the ATF. They're still investigating, but that didn't have anything to do with Erica," he said.

"Does your wife have any relatives? A sister, maybe?" Alma asked.

"No. She was an only child and her parents died while she was in high school. Some freak accident that set the whole place on fire. Erica felt guilty she was the only one who survived, even after all these years." Foster turned his attention back to the chief. "I don't understand. You said you had a good idea of who did this. Why are you wasting time with me when you could be building a case against them?"

Cree stepped into the grieving husband's peripheral vision so as to not take him by surprise. "Mr. Foster, we've run background checks, searched financials and phone records, gone through missing person reports across the country and have sent your wife's DNA to the state forensic lab for testing." He shrugged as though there were no other explanation. Because there wasn't. "Erica Harmon doesn't exist."

Color drained from Foster's face, his mouth parting slightly. "What the hell does that mean?" He shoved out of his seat, and the chair tipped backward. "Is this some sick game to you? Erica was my wife. You ask anyone in Ouray who knows us. I've known her since she was a senior in high school living out of her car. You test my baby's DNA. I'm telling you Erica…" Disbelief brought Foster's hands to his head. "No. This isn't… This isn't happening. Her name was Erica Harmon. We've been together going on ten years." He pulled his wallet from his back pocket and flipped it open to a photo taken sometime in the past few years, if Cree had to guess. "She loved me. She loved Ethan. She wouldn't leave us. She wouldn't lie to us."

"Even if it was to protect you?" Alma asked.

Silence filled the too-small room. Tears streaked down Foster's face, and Cree collected the tissue box from the chief's desk. He took the offering, still staring at the photo of him and his wife. Acceptance eased the pain in the man's gaze. "She'd never talk about her childhood. No matter how many times I asked. I wanted to do a family recipe book, you know. Something we could pass down to Ethan when he was older and ready to move out on his own. He could learn about his family and how to cook from all his ancestors. We both picked our favorite recipes, but Erica… She wouldn't write down the stories behind them, like it was too painful to remember." Foster swept his hand under his nose. "She'd have nightmares about the fire, the one that killed her parents. Whenever I asked her about them, she'd change the subject. After a handful of times, I stopped asking." He swiped at his face, then replaced his wallet in his back pocket. "She was still having nightmares up until she disappeared. I never told her she talked in her sleep."

"What did she say?" Chief Ford asked.

"The same thing every time, a name," Foster said. "Christine."

Cree set the tissue box in front of Foster on the desk and took the opportunity to study Alma for a reaction. Her move to record the admission in her notebook was quick and efficient, a testament to the detail-oriented reserve officer he'd come to respect. "Does that name mean anything to you?"

"No. She never talked about anyone named Christine." Foster reached into another pocket, this time in the front of his jeans. "But after you'd told me what happened to Erica the other day, I mean…my wife… I started going through her things to figure out what I needed to keep to pass down to Ethan and what I could donate. I found this with a small bag of clothes under her side of the bed. I thought it was just in case of emergency, you know? Like those preppers do. If the house caught fire, and we had to make a quick escape…" He pulled a black flip phone free. "She'd packed outfits for each of us."

Chief Ford stood from behind his desk and tugged open the top drawer. Extracting a pair of latex gloves, he snapped them over his hands before taking the evidence Foster offered. "This isn't Erica's?"

"No." Foster shook his head, a habit at this point. "We both have smartphones. I don't know why she thought she needed to hide it from me. I couldn't even find a charger for it."

Cree examined the phone from beside the chief. "Old phones like this are harder to track." He pointed at the notification on the small exterior screen. "Says there's a voice mail. Did you listen to it?"

Foster scrubbed a hand down his face. "Not yet."

Chief Ford flipped the face of the device open and held down the number 1 to dial voice mail and hit the speaker button. *You have one new message.* Static filtered through the dated speakers.

"Did you think you could run from me, Danny? Did you think I wouldn't find you? I have the resources of the entire United States government at my fingers. You don't get to have your happily-ever-after with your family. It's my turn."

The call ended.

Danny? Cree raised his gaze to Alma, but from the set of her expression, she was soaking up everything she could from the call. Only the longer he studied her, the more shaking he noted in her hand. Just as he had last night.

Message received at 8:07 a.m., April fourth, the electronic voice reported.

"April fourth?" Foster's defeated expression drained as a bolt of energy lit up his eyes. "That's the day Erica disappeared."

"If she was in possession of the phone, it stands to reason the message was meant for her." Chief Ford flipped the phone closed and bagged it into evidence. "Do you know who Danny is?"

"I don't know anyone by that name," Foster said.

"Could be short for Danielle. Danny might be a nickname." Cree offered his hand to shake. "Thank you for your help, Mr. Foster. We're going to get a warrant for the phone's records. With any luck, we'll be able to trace the number the call came from and go from there."

"Just...find who did this. For my son." Foster hesitated, then took hold of Cree's hand. "Please."

"We'll call as soon as we find something. Thank you again for coming down." The chief stood, rolling his gloves from his hands, and directed Foster out the door and from the station.

Cree followed on their heels only as far as the chief's office door and closed it behind them, giving Alma a minute to collect herself. "What is it?"

"It was her. The voice mail." Alma lowered her voice and craned her head over her shoulder to get a lock on Chief Ford. She wasn't the type to keep information from her commanding officer, especially concerning an investigation, but she was the type to hide how that voice mail had rocked her. "I recognize the voice."

"You're sure?" he asked.

"It was the last thing I thought I'd hear before I

die." Alma fisted her uninjured hand in front of her on a strong inhale. "I'll never forget it. I don't think our victim did, either."

Chapter Eleven

We're sorry. The number you have dialed has been disconnected. Please check—

Alma ended the call. The calls received log in the phone Travis Foster recovered from his home listed only a single number. The incoming voice mail. No saved contacts. No fingerprints to match to their victim. Nothing to give them a clue as to why Erica Harmon—or whoever she used to be—had been on the run or why she'd kept a connection to her old life. If she believed her life was in danger, why keep a separate phone at all? To use in case she and Travis Foster and the baby had to leave? Phones like this had become obsolete, but they weren't difficult to attain. Why this phone? Why hide it from her husband?

She twisted her hand and nudged at the locket sitting open on Cree's small dining table with the end of her pen. *Did you think you could run from me?* Alma closed her eyes against the last image of her abductor at the edge of the trees, seconds before the bomb strapped to her midsection was scheduled to detonate. *You're going to want to keep your eye on that clock, Officer Majors.* It was the same voice. She'd known the moment it had filtered through the speaker, and every cell in her body had screamed for her to run. She imagined she'd have the same reaction if her ex-husband decided to reenter her life. "One issue at a time, Majors."

"Any luck?" Cree stepped into the narrow hallway with a thick shower towel draped across his shoulders. Droplets of water ran along the tendons in his neck and darkened the color of his hair.

Alma pulled herself straighter and set the phone on the table. "No. Nothing. Whatever number the killer called Erica from is disconnected."

"Not surprising." He maneuvered into the kitchen and reached for one of the mugs stacked next to the coffeepot. In seconds, he'd filled two cups and crossed the short distance between them to offer one of them to her. "According to that message, whoever's behind this has the resources of the US government at their disposal, and from what I've seen and what you've said, she's well-trained. She wouldn't want something as simple as a phone number connecting back to her."

"Easton's working on who the number was registered to before it was disconnected, but even with a warrant, it's going to take time." She set her pen over the edge of her notepad, mesmerized by the single name written in the center of the page. Christine.

"You know, I've been trying not to let myself think about what happened apart from what was important to put into my statement, but when I heard her voice on that voice mail, I remembered something when she mentioned her resources."

Cree took a seat opposite her, the table barely big enough to seat two adults. His knees brushed against hers for the briefest of moments, and a fraction of the spark she'd felt when he kissed her exploded through her. "I'm listening."

"She said she'd met you before." Alma memorized his expression, waiting for any change. The slight narrowing of his eyes wasn't enough to reveal the internal dialogue going on behind those forest green eyes, but she liked to think he was as transparent with her as she'd been with him.

"Did she say where? When?" he asked.

"No. She was mostly focused on making sure I didn't walk away from those woods alive." She tramped down a shudder, tracing the rim of her mug with one finger. "But if the killer is telling the truth on that voice mail—and I can't think of a reason she'd lie about having the US government behind her—then I'm inclined to believe the two of you might've crossed paths professionally."

Cree leaned back in his seat. He blew out an exaggerated breath, directing his gaze out the small bay window lighting the breakfast nook. "It's possible. She said she met me. Not that she knew me?"

"Yes." She took a sip of her coffee, willing her nerves to settle.

"She has experience with explosives. She's confident in her skills, which leads me to believes she's most likely professionally trained." He scrubbed a hand down his face. "If she's a peer, there are any number of ways we could've met. Our initial training consists of engineering, chemistry and explosives. I got mine in the army, but there are dozens of bureaus that train bomb techs. FBI, ATF, other branches of the military, law enforcement. Even if we were to narrow down who she works for, I'm required to train with other counties and stay up-to-date through continuing education courses across the country to keep my certifications. She could've been in any one of those classes."

The pick-me-up she'd hoped to get from her coffee failed. Another dead end. Her attention went back to the notes she'd taken during Travis Foster's interview and the frenzied circle around a single word. Christine. "We have a potential name. According to the victim's husband, Erica frequently had nightmares where she recalled the name Christine. If this is who she'd been running from all these years, it's possible we can narrow the search. Does it sound familiar at all?"

"No, but I still have contacts in Larimer County. I can start asking around. If there was a Christine in any one of our trainings, they'd have a record of the registration." Cree took another pull from his mug, that too intense gaze weighing on her. No judgment. No expectations. Just curiosity. "Did you get any sleep?"

"A little." A lie. Alma twisted the base of her mug into the table. Exhaustion had caught up with her for a couple of hours, but her brain was still trying to process the details of this investigation. "I was going through old arson cases most of the night."

"The fire Erica Harmon's parents supposedly died in when she was in high school." Admiration bled into his voice, and the hairs on the back of her neck stood on end. "We're not even sure of the victim's real name. Did you have any luck?"

"Not really. There are too many unknown variables. City, victim identity, when the fire took place, location. I plugged in both 'Danielle' and 'Christine', but there were no hits. As an archaeologist I trained to trace the smallest detail back to the beginning. I got really good at it, too, but this case is nothing but a bunch of dead ends." A humorless laugh punctured through the gloom in her mood. "I did, however, find something interesting when I looked under your bed."

Cree leaned back in his seat and closed his eyes. "Oh no."

"Oh yes." The tension she'd been holding on to since walking through the front door last night eased as she reached down near her feet. Alma grabbed the collection of soft yarn and metallic needles. "I'm really interested in what you're doing here." She arranged the deep green yarn on one side of the table and positioned the knitting needles in both hands. "From the look of it, you've started a...scarf? You could stand to tighten up the tension here on one end, but you've got a good start."

Buried embarrassment twitched at the corners of his mouth. Cree kept his voice even, those calloused fingers itching to rip the project out of her hands, but he held himself back. It seemed he wasn't going to let her get the best of him. Yet. "The winters here are harsher than in Loveland. I needed a scarf, and my grandfather taught me to do things myself instead of going to a store to buy what I needed. And if you must know, knitting keeps my hands strong enough to do my job."

"Your grandfather taught you to knit?" she asked.

"Crochet and sewing, too. Though every once in a while, he'd get the crochet hook caught in his beard and throw the hook across the room." A wisp of a smile softened his features. "He considered himself a Jack of all trades."

"He sounds like someone I would've liked." She meant it. Because without the dedication and love of Cree's grandfather, Cree wouldn't be here now. And she didn't want to imagine a world without him. Not anymore. As much as she didn't trust herself to make the right decision under pressure or to look past the masks people presented to the world, she trusted him.

"He would've liked you, too," he said. "You're a lot like him. Hardworking, cautious, definitely not one to let others make decisions for herself." His laugh permeated her senses, filling her with a lightness she'd hadn't felt in years. "He was a good man, someone who gave to the community as much as he took. Tough, though. You never wanted to find yourself on the wrong end of one of his lectures. To him, everything was life and death. You did what you were told or you died."

"Sounds like he cared about you very much." Heat worked up her neck and into her face. Her parents had supported her, loved her, but she'd mostly gone through life on her own. Always looking for the next adventure, the next dig site, the next research proposal, and they'd given her that independence. When her ex had come along, they'd gotten married so quickly: Alma had considered their relationship an adventure too, and her parents had thrown their support behind her. But when she'd filed for divorce, they hadn't understood why she couldn't try to fix it, why she'd had to leave, why she was giving up. They'd meant well, she knew that, but the way Cree talked about his grandfather... She envied the kind of support that really mattered.

She ran her thumb along the three inches of unequal stitches he'd knitted and raised the project higher. The partial scarf caved under her touch, and she found herself imagining what it would feel like complete. "Can you teach me?"

"You want me to teach you to knit?" Cree asked. "Isn't that already one of those superpowers you inherited from your *abuela*?"

"Not yet, but I have a feeling you could show her a thing or two." Alma pinned the project in her uninjured hand and slid out of her seat. Setting the mass of yarn on the table in front of him, she scooted her chair closer and sat. "I'm all ears, and one hand. So go slow."

His resulting smile cut through the last of her defenses and opened an entire realm of possibilities she hadn't considered before she'd taken on this case. An entire future. "All right. First things first. You have to learn how to cast the yarn onto the needles." He stripped his work in progress free and handed over both needles. "It's going to be hard with only one hand, but as long as we work together, nothing can stop us."

THEY'D ONLY KNITTED a few rows when Alma's phone rang with an incoming call from Chief Ford. She'd excused herself to take it in his bedroom and left him to finish off what they'd started together. Despite Alma's superhuman breadth of skills, knitting hadn't been one of them. Cree gathered the yarn and needles and shoved them in the junk drawer in the kitchen. Even after he'd realized their combined efforts weren't enough to save the scarf, he'd enjoyed the few minutes they'd taken together, the partnership they'd built.

It hadn't been enough for her to show him the kind of dedication and sympathy it took to investigate a case like this, she had to go convince him this town belonged in his future. Whether that future included Alma, he wasn't sure, but he knew what he wanted. He knew what he was ready to give up to get it, too.

He unplugged his cell from the charger on the kitchen counter where he'd left it the night before. One missed call. He tapped on the notification, and his phone instantly dialed his CO's number. Two rings. Three. The line picked up.

"Wasn't sure you'd call me back." Glen May didn't make small talk. With the entire county and two other city departments to rope into cooperation under his purview, the man valued his time over everything else, and he didn't mince words. It was one of the qualities that had rocketed May from a patrol officer into the county's good graces enough for him to run for sheriff. He got the job done—no heroics, no frills—even when one of his technicians had gone off the deep end.

"Sheriff, it's been a while." Cree didn't know what else to say. May wasn't the kind to drop a line without good reason, and Cree was still on leave. Something had happened.

"Heard you been chasing a firecracker down there in Battle Mountain. Four bombs in as many days." A chair squeaked on the other side of the line, and Cree's brain automatically constructed the image of May behind his desk twirling that mustache at one corner. "That chief you got down there called me to verify you're one of my techs. Didn't really know what to say to him considering our last conversation, but I vouched for you."

Cree directed his attention down the hall, catching Alma's warped voice from the other side of the door. It had been four days since that initial explosion in the gulch—the one that had nearly killed Alma in the process—and he felt just as lost as he did then. "I've got your thank-you note right here, Glen. Just need to stop by the post office."

"We both know that's a lie." The sheriff's deep laugh resonated through the phone, and a twinge of homesickness barked up Cree's spine. While he hadn't thought much about going back to his life, there were some things he'd missed. Including the old man who made Cree imagine himself forty years from now. "Listen, I know you're working that investigation in the bomber around those parts. That Ford fellow says you've been doing some solid work, but it's time to come home, Cree."

"What do you mean?" he asked.

"I mean I've been holding your job for you for eight months while you get your head right, which I was happy to do after what happened at the county commissioners meeting, but now I hear you're investigating a bomber out of your jurisdiction." May lowered his voice. "I know you. I know you feel obligated to offer assistance given your background and the fact you're probably the only one capable of helping those people, but Battle Mountain isn't a place guys like you make a career. You're the best tech I've got. Let them sort out their own problems."

The phone protested under Cree's grip. "And if I want to see this case through?"

"The mayor's office wanted me to let you know how much they appreciate your service and what you've been through since the bombing," May said. "They know you're a man they can depend on the next time a bunch of ecoterrorists decide to take matters into their own hands, and I agreed. You're a hell of a tech with the skills to do a lot of good here, but their fuses are getting short, Cree. I can't hold them off anymore. They made their decision clear. Either you come back to the squad or your career in explosive ordnance is over."

"That's… That's not… Wow." Disbelief burned through him, almost as hot as the blisters along the backs of his hands.

"Come on, man. It's an easy choice. This is your career we're talking about. Tell me you're not actually considering giving all that up." May's desk chair protested under his weight again. "Now, I've been patient enough, and I can't make any more excuses as to why you're not here doing the work."

"I just…thought I had more time." He turned his back to the bedroom door. This wasn't why he'd called his CO back. Cree closed his eyes to regain a fraction of focus. "I don't really know what to say other than I'll have to think about it."

"Well, don't make it sound so dreary. Your life is here, son. Your team, your career, they're waiting for you to get your head back in the game." The sheriff's voice dropped into manipulative territory. "Isn't that what you want?"

Cree didn't know. On one hand he'd found a better version of himself in this small town—found Alma—and on the other, the life he'd spent years building, one where he could prove himself. "Give me twenty-four hours. Okay? Until then, I need your help. Do you remember any recruits or agents that go by the name Christine? Someone who would've interacted with our squad in the past few years."

"Does Christine have a last name?" May asked.

"If she does, I can't remember what it is or what she looks like. All I have is a first name." Cree's energy spiked from impatience.

"I have hundreds of people come through here a year who interact with the squad. Deputies, witnesses, federal agents. Bound to be a few named Christine. Does this have to do with your firecracker down there?" The sheriff's tone leveled off enough for Cree to understand the man had already gotten his answer.

"I'm not sure yet," he said. "Might be nothing."

"Let's see what we've got here." Slow typing bled through the line as Cree envisioned May balancing the phone receiver between his shoulder and bulbous jaw as he pecked at the keyboard. "The only Christine I recall is from a training seminar we hosted about two years ago. ATF agent. I've got her card around here somewhere. Feisty, redheaded thing who seemed to have a problem with everyone she talked to, including me."

"Maybe it was because you called her a feisty, redheaded thing instead of calling her by her name like a normal person." Cree pressed his phone harder against his ear as the call threatened to cut out.

"Agent Christine Freehan," May said. "According to this, she presented a seminar on HMEs about four years ago."

"Homemade explosives. I remember. We identified precursor chemicals used in homemade devices in a blind test. We had to figure out the compositions without any direction." Cree filtered through the dozens of courses he'd taken over the years but still couldn't get a visual of the agent in charge. The Alcohol, Tobacco, Firearms and Explosives Bureau didn't post their agents' photos or information for public consumption, but it was possible he could get access through his ATF contact. "Send me the agent's contact information. I'll get a hold of her myself. Thanks, Glen."

Cree disconnected before May had a chance to manipulate an answer about coming back to Loveland, and turned for the bedroom at the end of the hall. He nearly ran straight into Alma. "Hey, I might have a lead on the name Christine. Turns out there's an ATF agent who taught a continuing education course to my squad a couple years ago…" He noted the lack of color in Alma's face and the strain of her uninjured hand around her phone. He braced himself, his own grip too tight as every muscle in his body hardened with battle-ready tension. "What's going on?"

"I'm needed back at the station," she said.

"What happened?" A flood of possibilities hiked his blood pressure higher.

"That was the chief on the phone." She motioned behind her. She avoided his gaze, as though she were trying to keep herself together. "There's been another attack."

"When?" Blood drained down the length of his body. He hadn't heard the explosion, hadn't heard emergency response. No. It hadn't been a bomb. The chief wouldn't have called Alma on her cell for that. "Where?"

"In Ouray. Last night." Her voice shook, and Cree closed the distance between them.

Ouray. He tossed his cell on the couch and reached

for her, but Alma's quick dodge triggered a flood of rejection and confusion. "Travis Foster."

"The unit assigned to keep an eye on Foster's home was attacked. When they came around, they realized someone had broken in. Sergeant Hale responded to the scene. When he arrived, he found the front door smashed in and the place torn apart." Her shoulder rose on a shaky inhale. "Foster was on the floor, unconscious. Someone beat him to within an inch of his life. Chief Ford is headed there now. From what he was able to get from Sergeant Hale, it looks as though Foster fought back."

"Do they think it's the same person who killed Erica Harmon? The bomber? The killer wasn't happy with the way her sister died, she had to go after Erica's family?" He wasn't sure why he expected Alma to have any of the answers. She'd been just as blindsided at this development as he was. Then a single thought iced in his mind. "What about the baby?"

The muscles in her throat worked overtime to swallow. "He's gone."

Chapter Twelve

The Amber Alert had gone out hours ago, but Alma hadn't heard any response. Travis Foster and Erica Harmon's baby was out there, and they had no idea where to even start looking.

She glazed through the latest report blurring in front of her. No matter how many cases she'd gone through, Alma couldn't find one that linked back to a couple who'd died in a fire, leaving two teenage daughters behind. Not in the past decade, at least. No mention of a Danny or Danielle. Nothing to link the ATF agent Cree suspected of having a hand in this case. Not even a recent photo of their victim other than the one Travis Foster had used to file the missing person report.

She swept her hair back away from her face and scanned the empty station. Chief Ford had gone over to Ouray to assist at the scene of the break-in, and Easton had been needed at the rehab center for his fiancée's therapy. Macie was on break for the next twenty minutes, leaving Alma to man the phones, and she wasn't sure where Cree had gone. She didn't need to keep tabs on her partner, but there'd been a distinct separation between them since learning of the break-in and abduction. Her gut tightened as she buried the urge to overassess the phone call she'd overheard with Cree's CO. It wasn't her business whether or not he stayed in Battle Mountain, but for the first time since escaping the gulch and that first explosion, she wasn't just physically alone, she felt alone.

Alma hauled herself away from her desk and pushed her hips forward to counter the ache building in her lower back. Her boots skimmed across the old carpeting as she made her way into the break room, Macie's headset firmly squeezing her head on either side. Gripping the coffeepot handle, she reached for a clean mug and tipped the pot to one side. Empty. "Damn it."

There was still too much they didn't know. Year of the fire, location, victims' names. Erica Harmon had been living a lie. She'd run from whatever life she'd had to escape the person she blamed for the house fire—even going as far to change her name—but it hadn't been enough. The killer had caught up to her, had made sure no one would interrupt the sick game put into play.

She replaced the pot on the stand and cleaned out the grounds from the filter. Within a couple of minutes, the scent of fresh coffee chased back the apprehension set up under her skin. Bubbling water popped from inside the machine as she considered her next steps. Silverton's bomb squad had collected as much evidence as they could from the primary scene and the electronics store, but without confirmation from the shard of bone concerning the victim's identity from the forensic lab, she had nothing.

"Hey. Thought you might need a pick-me-up from Caffeine and Carbs down the street." Cree leaned against the doorframe leading into the break room with a white paper bag in his hand, every inch the man she'd grown comfortable with these past few days. She hadn't heard him come through the back door, having been too overwhelmed with a never-ending loop of questions in her head. "I told the guy behind the counter that I was heading over to the station, and he sent along a chocolate glazed doughnut just for you."

"Reagan is good at remembering customer favorites, but I think he keeps notes to make sure he gets it right." She wished something as simple as a doughnut could bring her out of this...emptiness that wouldn't leave. She'd been here before. After her divorce. She'd spent so long fighting to survive, to move forward, that she wasn't prepared for what happened after she'd escaped, after the charges had been filed, after the arrest had been made. She wasn't prepared for the hollowness and loneliness on the other side, even knowing she was free to do whatever she wanted with her life. This job had helped pull her from the depths, and Cree… He'd given her the strength to keep herself from falling back in. Only now his career was at stake back in Loveland, and there was nothing in this sleepy small town that could compare. "Thanks."

He moved to set the bag on the counter beside her but didn't come any closer. "Everything okay?"

"Yeah. It's just…" She shook her head to pull herself out of what-if territory. No. Now wasn't the time to ask him about his decision. The case. The bomber. Travis Foster's missing baby. That was all that mattered. Not her, not him, or any theory of the future. "The shard of bone the EMT pulled from my shoulder is the key to all of this, but without something to compare it to, we have nothing."

"Travis Foster supplied direct reference samples from Erica's toothbrush and hairbrush, as well as a biological family member reference sample from the baby," he said.

"All that means is we've confirmed what we already knew: the woman we know as Erica Harmon died in that bombing. But who was Erica Harmon?" Alma folded her uninjured arm across her midsection. "She changed her name, went on the run. For all we know, she could've had cosmetic work to change her features. The photo used to file the missing person report might be useless, and I haven't been able to find anything on a Danny or Danielle or Christine in all those old arson case files."

"I put in a word with a buddy who went to work for ATF earlier this year. He doesn't operate out of her field office, so he's not familiar with Agent Christine Freehan personally, but he's heard her name through the grapevine. Apparently she's the kind of investigator who does whatever it takes to get an arrest. Rumors include bribes and threats, although the bureau hasn't been able to find anything solid to suspend her or investigate. She's good at her job, one of the best in her field, and she's got the confidence and the training to go with it." Cree waited for her to answer, but none of what he'd said put them a step closer. "Silverton's squad is finished processing the primary scene. They recovered more fragments of bone and some tissue. Only problem is, as individual pieces, they don't lead anywhere we haven't already been."

"Individual pieces." Alma shoved away from the counter. Her heart rate ticked up a notch as a dose of adrenaline dumped into her veins. There'd been times in the field during a dig she'd unearth a fracture of pottery or a sun stone that had been damaged over the course of thousands of years. One piece. That was all she needed to complete the puzzle. "That's it."

Cree hesitated bringing his to-go coffee cup to his mouth. "What's it?"

"Individual pieces are a good start, but until we have the whole picture, we're just going in circles." Unpocketing her cell, she rounded back into the station's lobby and sat behind Macie's two-tiered expansive desk. She rolled the desk chair from one side to the other and located the tacked contact list pinned to a homemade corkboard. She knocked over a bottle of bright nail polish as she skimmed her finger down the list and switched her phone into her uninjured hand to dial.

"Okay. And by whole picture, you're talking about the victim?" Cree asked. "You said it yourself, the victim might've had cosmetic surgery to alter her appearance. If that's the case, what will the whole picture accomplish if we don't know what she looked like in the first place?"

"Cosmetic surgery doesn't alter bone structure." Her breath shallowed as a hint of the joy she'd found in uncovering Mexico's lost heritage boiled to the surface. "The victim's skull might be in pieces, but if we can reconstruct it using tissue depth markers based on her race, sex and approximate age, we'll have something we can run a search for to give us Erica Harmon's original identity."

"Battle Mountain doesn't have a forensic artist," he said.

"No, but they do have the next best thing." Alma hit dial. "An archaeologist." Bringing the phone to her ear, she waited for the line to pick up, Cree in the wings of her peripheral vision. The line connected. "Dr. Miles, it's Officer Majors. Have you received all of the bone fragments recovered from the bombing scene yet?"

"They were just delivered. I haven't been able to do a complete examination yet, though. They're still in their evidence bags." Dr. Chloe Miles had run to Battle Mountain to hide from the killer desperate to keep her from exposing him for malpractice in the death of a patient and straight into Chief Ford's protection. The thirty-something coroner's background lay in cardiothoracic surgery and saving lives, but with her past behind her, the mother-to-be had reinvented herself as a key asset of the town. Without her, the department wouldn't have been able to bring down not one but two serial killers focused on tearing Battle Mountain apart. Now Alma needed her help. "Why?"

"Great. I need you to start separating the bones of the victim's skull from the rest of the fragments." She raised her gaze to Cree. "It's going to take some time, but I think I have a way to identify her."

"I hope that's true." Dr. Miles's doubt bled through the line and set up residence in Alma's bones. "But if anyone can help me put her back together, it's you. Meet me at my office as soon as you can, and we can get started."

The line disconnected.

She pocketed her phone and stood, all too aware

of Cree's proximity. There'd been a shift between them in the time he'd ended his call with his CO and now. She didn't blame him for wanting to give in to the temptation to leave. Given the choice, she never would've walked away from the career she'd loved, and he deserved to be happy, even if it meant him leaving. She could already feel herself pulling away in the time that had passed between that call and now. Which didn't make sense. He hadn't told her he wanted to go back to Loveland, but her instinct to detach, to protect herself from losing anything more, had already taken hold. "I need to get over there. The sooner Dr. Miles and I can start reconstructing the skull, the sooner we'll have a fresh face to search for. With any luck, we'll get a hit."

"I'll grab my stuff," he said.

"That's okay. You stay." Her voice hiked an octave, giving away the emotional tsunami pummeling her control from every direction. "Macie's not back from her break yet. Someone needs to cover the phones in case the Amber Alert pays off." She headed for the front door. "I'll call you with any updates."

"Alma, wait." He reached for her, but thought better of making contact, which she appreciated. "Did something happen? You've barely said a word since we left the apartment, and when you do... Did I do something to upset you?"

Her heart threatened to shatter right there in the

middle of the station. Alma gripped her backpack strap to give herself a distraction, a reason not to commit to the moment, as she'd done so many times before. "No, Cree. You didn't do anything. I just..." She deflated. "I overheard your phone call with your CO. I know your job with Larimer County's bomb squad is at risk, and I think you should go back."

HE DIDN'T KNOW what to say to that, what to think. Cree fought to keep his breathing even as he replayed her words over in his mind, but there was no point in denying the truth. He tossed his empty coffee cup and slid his hands into his pockets. "The mayor got word I'm involved in the investigation here. Seems they don't like the idea of me working a case out of my jurisdiction when I'm supposed to be on medical leave."

"So your CO gave you an ultimatum. Come back or lose your career." The mask Alma had slowly surrendered over the past few days had set back in place, and suddenly Cree didn't recognize the woman standing in front of him. She peeled the dispatcher headset from her head and set it on the desk. "Sounds like an easy decision to me."

Pressure built behind his sternum as he studied her. The warmth he'd grown to rely on over the course of this investigation was gone. What he now saw was the detached deputy he'd met at the primary scene, the one who'd taken on the weight of the world and shut down any possibility of letting someone close. "Is it?"

"Cree, I've walked away from a career. Something I'd spent my entire life training for, something I loved with all my heart, and I let someone take it from me. I don't want to be the person you resent because you felt like you had no other choice." She shifted her weight from one leg to the other. Antsy. Anxious. Nothing like the woman he'd gotten to know while they'd worked together to knit a scarf or pretended to escape the hospital. "I know you said you could see yourself giving up the life you built back in Loveland, but we both know Battle Mountain's department isn't going to keep you happy. I mean, look at this place." She diverted her attention to the stained beige walls. "We're barely functioning as it is. There are no days off because we're so short-staffed. There's no pension. There's nowhere to go here."

"Did you consider none of that mattered to me?" Cree had respected her need for space all this time, but it hadn't done either of them a damn bit of good. She wanted him gone? Fine. He could deal with that, but hiding behind their insecurities wasn't going to satisfy the pain carving through him. "Did you ever consider this town has become more than an escape for me? That I might want to stay because I've gotten to know the people? That my feelings for my partner outweighed any reason I had to leave?"

She didn't answer. Didn't even seem to breathe. There was no crack in the armor she'd donned because she'd gotten too good at living life behind it. What had happened with her ex-husband, the crumbling of her marriage, had served only one purpose: to protect her from having to feel anything ever again.

"You don't really want me to go back, Alma. I think you're scared. I think you have feelings for me, too. I saw it when you let me hold you on my couch and when you trusted I would find you in those woods. You're afraid to get hurt again. Like your husband hurt you. You're terrified of someone else getting close, someone who could potentially hurt you, and that kind of risk just isn't worth taking." Anger charged through his veins, and with it rejection, pain and worthlessness. The fight drained from his shoulders and face. "This isn't about whether or not I try to salvage my life in Loveland. It's that I'm not worth the risk, am I?"

A line of tears glistened in her eyes, but from the look of how tight she'd clamped her teeth, Alma wouldn't let them fall. "No. You're not."

Her words hit him as solidly as a sucker punch to the gut, but there wouldn't be any taking them back. It hadn't been enough to give her space or a safe place to hide during the investigation, to earn her trust and make her laugh. Cree wouldn't ever be capable of getting through that hardened exterior.

Not as long as Alma fell victim to the fear of her past. The realization punctured through his chest and stole the air from his lungs. He'd been willing to leave his old life behind, to start something new with her, but it hadn't been enough. He wasn't sure it ever would be. "You don't deserve to live like this, Alma. There are people here who care about you, who would do anything to make you feel safe and put your happiness before theirs. I like to think I could've been one of them."

"But that's the thing. None of them have survived what I have. None of them could understand I have to do this on my own." Alma swept the back of her hand across her face. "What we had these past few days… It was always going to end like this. I'm just cutting the root before it strangles us both."

His gut twisted. She was a domestic abuse survivor. He knew she was planning ten steps ahead to survive multiple possibilities, but this wasn't the way he'd imagined their partnership dissolving. If anything, he'd been testing himself to ensure he was enough for her when she needed him. Truth was, he wasn't, just as he hadn't been enough to save those people who'd died in the conference bombing eight months ago, and he would have to live with that weight for the rest of his life. "Understood, Officer Majors."

She flinched at his use of her title and last name, but the forced detachment did nothing for him.

"For what it's worth, I thought we made a good team." He pointed to the front desk. "I'll cover the phones until Macie gets back from her break. Good luck with your reconstruction of the skull. I hope you find what you're looking for."

Her rough exhale filled his ears a split second before she turned her back on him and headed out the front doors.

Skimming his fingers across Macie's desk, he took up the dispatcher headset and fit it into place before taking his seat. Tension lined his jaw, but no amount of control released the pressure building in the space beneath his ears. A headache bloomed behind both eyes, and the text on the computer monitor blurred. The past four days had thrown him from one end of the emotional spectrum to the other, leaving him unbalanced and high-strung. The grief from having to walk away from not only this case or this town but the first person he'd felt closest to since his grandfather had passed drilled through his chest. The coffee he'd slugged raged in revenge. Where the hell was Macie?

The station line rang in his ear.

The square yellow indicator on the nineties-era phone flickered, and Cree hit the button. "911, what's your emergency?"

"That baby, the one from the Amber Alert on my phone, I think I just saw him." The distressed voice on the other line didn't sound familiar, but Cree's attention hung on every word. "Please. You have to send someone."

"Okay, ma'am. Can you tell me where you are and if the child is with someone?" He reached for the pen cup near the dispatch monitor and pulled a hot pink glitter pen from the collection of the rainbow assortment. Biting the cap off, he waited for an answer. "Ma'am?"

The call disconnected one second short of the system logging name and location details.

Confusion arced through him. The computer automatically logged the recent call and recorded the call back number. Dropping the pen, he hit the number to reopen the line. It rang twice. Three times. Voice mail picked up on the other end after the fourth, but the automated message failed to identify the caller. It did however give the computer time to narrow the phone's GPS. Cree surveyed the map on the screen. Dispatching software was able to narrow down a caller's location to within fifty feet, but this… "That can't be right."

The call had originated right outside the station doors.

Another indicator on the screen filled in the caller's name, and a flood of clarity washed through him.

Erica Harmon.

It hadn't been a concerned citizen on the other end of the line.

It had been the killer.

Cree reached for the radio on the other side of the desk and pressed the push-to-talk button. He shoved to his feet and headed straight back to the chief's office. In a matter of seconds, he'd located Chief Ford's backup weapon secure in the bottom drawer of the man's desk, then headed for the front of the station. "All units, be advised, 10-33 in immediate need of assistance. Battle Mountain Police Station. Bomber is in the vicinity—"

The glow of a red LED light beneath the chief's desk bled onto his boots, and he froze. His finger slipped from the push-to-talk button.

"Ford to dispatch, I missed that last part. Repeat." Chief Ford's voice echoed as though Cree were somewhere else, like static on the television set his parents used to own. Just out of reach.

Cree's knees popped as he crouched beneath the desk. His gaze instantly went to the countdown ticking silently from the four-stack of C4 duct-taped underneath the thick wood. His exhale slid up his throat.

"Dispatch, do you copy? Cree, what's going on over there?" Easton's voice threatened to distract him. The uneven tone suggested the deputy had gotten the hint and was hauling ass back to the station. "Officer Majors, do you copy? 10-33."

He peeled the tape free, one strand at a time, and cradled the device. C4 in and of itself was very stable. It needed that extra spark to ignite, but there was no telling how far the bomber had gone to ensure no one left the station alive this time. The same red wire coiled from the motherboard into the center of the C4. The caller had wanted to make sure someone was in the building. It hadn't been good enough to target Alma. She wanted to take out the entire department closing in. Fingers shaking, he registered the last minute and a half of the countdown as he tugged the coiling wire free from the explosive.

The clock stopped.

Nervous energy skittered across his shoulders as he set the entire thing on top of the desk. This was the only surviving explosive the bomber had left behind. He pulled an evidence bag from the chief's desk and wrapped the device as carefully as possible. No sudden movements.

The back door of the station swung open, heels clicking on the floor a few seconds after. "Honey, I'm home."

Macie.

"Back here." Cree slumped in the chair, his head pounding. The call outside the station had been a diversion. He ripped off the dispatch headset and tossed it on the desk as Macie rounded the corner, grip still tight around the handheld radio.

The bomber had been watching. Waiting.

"You really should treat other people's property with more respect." She moved into the office and reached for the headset. She knocked into the evidence bag and tilted it at an angle.

Cree wrapped his hand around hers, holding her completely still. A red glow bled into her already red hair from above, and he raised his gaze up. To the air vent directly above them. "Get out."

Macie pulled on her arm. "I don't know who the hell you think you are, Cree Gregson, but you don't get to talk to me that way—"

"Get out now!" He shoved out of the chair and pulled her along with him. A soft click registered just as they escaped the office.

And then there was fire.

Chapter Thirteen

The aftershock jarred the victim's skull fragments across the table.

Alma locked onto the edges to keep herself upright as fluorescent lights flickered overhead. Air stalled in her chest as she raised her gaze to Dr. Miles opposite. She'd felt an echo of that same punctured vibration the night she'd found this very victim at the bottom of the gulch. Releasing her grip on the table, she stripped out of the latex gloves and tossed them in the hazardous materials bin.

"What was that?" Dr. Miles fought to right herself.

"An explosion." Alma collected her utility belt and weapon from the counter and tightened them around her waist. They hadn't gotten far reassembling the victim's skull, but given enough time, there was a chance they could uncover exactly who'd died in that gulch. And who'd wanted her dead. She scanned the remains. The bomber had gone to extreme lengths to ensure Battle Mountain PD never properly identified this victim. No body, no crime. No way to connect the pieces back to the device or the person who had killed her. Alma unholstered her weapon as screams and frantic curiosity filtered through the steel door separating the medical examination room from the rest of the funeral home. She twisted the power knob on her radio, not realizing she hadn't turned it back on when she'd left the station and delegated her dispatch duties to Cree.

"Gregson, what the hell is going on? Answer me, damn it!" Chief Ford's voice panicked. "Officer Majors, 10-33, BMPD station. No response from dispatch. Please respond. Someone get on this damn radio!"

The station. Her gut filled in the blanks as the lights flickered again. Alma raised the radio to her mouth. "Majors responding. Possible 10-80." Explosion. She turned to the coroner. "All of these buildings on Main Street are connected. It's only a matter of time before the entire block goes up in flames. I need you to get everyone out."

"What about the evidence?" Dr. Miles moved around the end of the table. "We can't just leave her here to burn. We might never get an ID."

The overhead lights flickered again, and Alma backed toward the door. "Gather as much as you can. Just hurry!" She wrenched the door open and nearly crashed into the terrified funeral home director and his son. "Everyone outside. Go, go, go!"

Her heart rate shot into dangerous territory as Alma headed in the opposite direction of safety. She had to make sure there was no one left behind. The sales floor was clear, as was the break room and the small chapel. She charged to the front of the funeral home and out into the street. Dozens of open-mouthed citizens pointed to the raging fire consuming the building at the end of the street.

The station.

"Cree." A hard push from one of the townspeople knocked her injured shoulder back, and Alma doubled over to brace through the pain. Air hissed between her teeth. She forced herself to straighten. No on-scene support from her department. No sign of fire and rescue. All units had been sent up the mountain to battle the blaze. Even now, smoke threatened to black out the sky. She had to do this alone.

She grabbed a larger man's collar and pulled him into her chest. She couldn't remember his name in the moment, but she'd seen him several times along Main Street the past few months. Maybe one of Hopper's employees over at the hardware store. "I need you to get these people back away from the flames. Set up a perimeter, and do whatever it takes to make sure they don't cross it. Preferably on the other side of the street. Can you do that?"

The panicked, baby-faced man nodded before rushing to get the job done.

She scanned the crowd, echoes of gasps and cries

filling her ears, and targeted a group nearby. "You three." The young men turned horrified expressions toward her. "That fire is going to spread to the connecting buildings. I need you to help me get everyone out. We need to evacuate."

They followed her direction. "Two of you check that building next door, one of you with me. Move!" She wrenched open the front door to Caffeine and Carbs and crossed the checkered tile matching Greta's on Main. Illuminated pastry cases brightened the space. "Battle Mountain PD! Is anyone here?"

No answer.

Smoke tendrilled through the air-conditioning vents and set off the smoke detectors overhead. It lodged in her throat and revitalized the burn along the soft tissues of her mouth while the pierce worked to make her deaf. The fire was closing in, and they were running out of time. She motioned to the man with her. "Let's check the back."

"I can't... I can't do this. I'm sorry." He backed toward the door and triggered the bell over the frame.

"No, wait!" She took a single step after him, but it was no use. "Damn it." The smoke was growing thicker, the air hotter. Alma pressed the back of her wrist to her mouth and narrowed her gaze to see through the oncoming darkness. She moved around the display cases and down the hall leading to the back. "Is anyone here?"

A groan sounded from nearby, and she froze.

"Reagan?" She pumped her legs hard, scanning between each row of pan racks. A pair of legs materialized from beneath a large baking oven on wheels, dozens of small pies scattered across the floor. Instant recognition flared from the bright Hawaiian shirt pattern, and she collapsed to his side. "Reagan! Are you okay?" She set her hand in his to get a feel for a pulse.

"Alma…oven fell…blast…you gotta go…whole building…" The hippie-age baker mumbled through the rest of his warning. He most likely had a concussion, maybe some internal bleeding from the impact. Where the hell was fire and rescue? How far out were Chief Ford and Easton?

"You didn't even need your notes to remember my name." It didn't matter where everyone else was. She was here now. She had to be the one to help him. She released Reagan's hand and took position near his head to lift the oven. "Come on. I'm going to get you out of here. Push as hard as you can. I've got you."

Alma braced one shoulder against the oven, but it wouldn't move. The injury through her rotator cuff screamed in protest as she tried a second time. Still, it wouldn't move. Her eyes burned from the smoke curling through the bakery. Sweat pooled at the base of her spine and along her hairline, but she couldn't stop. "Reagan, we're going to have to work together here."

He didn't answer. The baker had lost consciousness, trapped beneath the behemoth he relied on to run his business. The temperature suddenly felt as though it'd gone up fifty degrees. She noted the paint bubbling from the opposite wall. Soon, the fire would break through and demolish everything in the bakery. Including her and Reagan. Alma swiped her hand across her face. She was the only chance he had of getting out of here alive. She wasn't going to leave him. She stripped the sling from her shoulder and tossed it aside. "We can do this. We can do this."

A scream clawed up her throat as she put everything she had into lifting the oven. Every muscle in her body burned with exertion. One centimeter at a time, the oven rose, but another weight piled on. The one she'd shouldered since her divorce.

Her grip faltered, and she struggled to reposition her hands for a better hold. It didn't matter how hard she'd committed herself to breaking free of the past, it had engrained itself into the fibers of her being, become part of her as Cree had said. The hurt she carried had given her an exit strategy out of getting too close, out of exposing herself again, and where had it left her? Here, in Caffeine and Carbs, trying to haul a burning hot oven off a victim of the most recent bombing. With no support, no backup, and no one but herself to blame. Because Cree had been right. She'd known it the moment he'd said the words. There were people here who cared about her, and she'd pushed them all away. Including him. The anxiety and loneliness she'd hoped to thwart by becoming part of a team had stayed buried for a long time, but now she realized it had been a ploy all along. A Band-Aid to the betrayal etched into her bones. Another scream tore from her. Her head ached with the tightness in her jaw. "Reagan, wake up! I need your help. I need…"

Cree.

His name settled at the tip of her tongue and intertwined with the fear taking hold. Fear she wasn't good enough for this work. Fear she'd die here. Fear she'd screwed up the connection between her and the only man who'd put her safety, needs and comfort above his own. Without complaint or resentment. Cree had punctured the bubble she'd created to separate herself from the rest of the world while making her stronger in the same breath. He'd tested her, pushed her to confront the pain she wanted to deny residence in her head, and been there on the other side when she couldn't do it alone. He'd given her all of him while expecting nothing in return, and she'd fallen in love with him because of it.

She loved him.

And it had scared her.

There wasn't any other explanation for why she'd severed their partnership. The mere thought of losing him had sent her into survival mode, and she'd run. Not physically. But emotionally, mentally. Because if she didn't have anything to lose, if she accepted she'd be alone, he couldn't hurt her. But she did have something to lose. Him. And she wasn't alone.

Cree had been in the station mere minutes before the explosion. Had he made it out alive? Had Macie come back from break? Sweat dripped from her chin as sizzling broke through the low ringing in her ears. A deep groan registered from above. The building was compromised. They had to get out of there. Alma dug her heels into the tiled floor.

"I can do this." She was getting Reagan out of here. She steadied her breathing and closed her eyes. Feeling for the balance between the oven and her momentum, she moved her hands closer into her chest, at risk of dropping the mammoth oven on Reagan all over again. But it didn't drop. She held strong, and with her mind clearer than it had been in days, she focused all of her energy into pushing it back. The wheels squeaked as they took the weight of the oven, and within seconds, Reagan was free. Alma could've collapsed right there, but the lick of flames breaking through the opposite wall said they'd run out of time.

She wrapped her fingers around Reagan's wrists and pulled him to the front of the bakery. She rammed her backside into the front door. "Help! Somebody! He needs an ambulance!"

"Mario. The refrigerator…he's in the refrigerator." Reagan's plea barely reached her ears, and she realized the baker wasn't talking about the cat she'd noticed prowling through the store. His assistant, Mario, wasn't staring back from the ocean of faces pushing the perimeter.

He was still inside.

A pair of residents ran to assist, and she handed Reagan off. A glance down the length of Main Street revealed the total loss of every shop south of the station. The entire complex was going to collapse. "Tell Chief Ford I'm headed back inside when he gets here. There's someone else in there." She wrenched the front door open on its hinges and ran straight toward the encroaching flames. Smoke interrupted her steady breathing, and her lungs spasmed in response. Covering her mouth and nose with her collar, she located the refrigerator. She swung the heavy metal door outward.

Empty.

"Don't worry, Officer Majors, Mario is safe," a voice said from behind. "You, on the other hand…"

Pain exploded through her skull and rocketed her forward. Alma hit the floor, her collar slipping from her mouth. Her vision blurred around the edges, but not enough to hide her attacker's identity as the woman relieved her of her weapon. Alma reached for her shield and unpinned it from her uniform, intent to use it as a weapon if needed. "You."

"Yeah." The bomber stepped on either side of Alma and clenched her collar in one hand. Arcing her hand back, she swung her gun a second time. "Me."

A HIGH-PITCHED RINGING pierced through what little consciousness he held on to.

Cree groaned under the weight of something solid and heavy on his chest, but the sound barely registered. He tried to haul his head away from whatever he'd landed on. In vain. Explosions of white light seared across his vision as he mentally scanned the length of his body. His toes had gone numb on his left foot. He stretched his jaw to get his ears to pop, but there wasn't any relief. Scrubbing a hand down his face, he spotted blood trickling from a laceration along the side of his hand.

Seconds distorted into confusing minutes. Flames licked the edges of what used to be the station's second floor straight above him. The call from outside the police station. The device he'd found in Chief Ford's office. Macie coming through the back door—each memory intertwined with the next until it was nothing but a mashup of fire, blood and pain. Cree kicked debris from his legs and set his hands beneath the beam to get out from under it. The second device. He hadn't found it until it'd been too late. And Macie... She'd been right next to him.

"Macie... Oh, hell." Cree wrapped one arm around his midsection in an attempt to keep his ribs from breaking completely. If they hadn't already. Ash rained from the floor above and mixed with the blood running into the crease of his elbow. The same ringing in his ears wouldn't let up as he hauled the beam off his chest with everything he had left. The wood protested before angling to his right. He swallowed the buildup of dryness in his mouth. The same terror he'd barely survived threatened to undo him all over again, but he couldn't hide this time. No matter how great the temptation, he couldn't run from this. Not again. "Macie, can you hear me?"

"I'm here." Movement honed his attention to a section of splintered wood and drywall ten feet away. Red hair coated in dust matted to a color-stricken and bloody face. "I'm okay. I think."

"We can't stay here." Pain sharpened his senses, and the ringing in his ear ceased. The building groaned above them. Water rushed from a broken pipe above but did nothing to douse the flames. "The bomb damaged the building's supports. It won't stay standing much longer."

"We should call 911." Macie swiped ash as she scanned the war zone they hadn't been fast enough to escape. Her hands shook. "But I'm not sure who would answer right now."

"Fire and rescue is still battling the forest fire." Cree dragged one arm behind him, his leg almost as useless, as he hobbled to stand. Dislocated shoulder, if he had to guess. "I'll get you out." He maneuvered through broken chunks of cement, drywall and tile and reached to help her to her feet.

"You owe me a new headset." Her words slurred there slightly at the end. The tremors quaking up her arms and into her neck signaled shock. She needed medical attention. Fast.

"Let's just focus on getting you out of here first." He secured a hand around her lower back to keep her upright and pulled her toward the only sliver of light visible in the whole damn place. From the layout of the building, he guessed the lobby door, but there were any number of things that could be messing with his sense of direction. Smoke thickened around them, but crawling through the debris for oxygen wasn't an option. They'd never make it out. "Lean on me."

"You're the one who can barely walk." Macie fisted her hands in his jacket. "Don't you mean you need to lean on me?"

The dispatcher's words were meant as sarcasm, but the sequence tunneled through the hollowness he'd lost himself in these past eight months. He'd run from Battle Mountain to hide, out of shame, out of guilt, out of embarrassment. As a highly trained bomb tech, he'd convinced himself he should've known the second device had been planted in the vent above the chief's office, just as he'd convinced himself he should've been able to disarm the bomb planted at that conference. The emptiness that had taken hold threatened to drag him beneath the surface as long as he lived, but while he'd believed he deserved it, he'd forgotten a key piece of the formula along the way. The same formula Macie wanted him to see now.

He didn't have to do this alone.

It had been easy enough to tell Alma to trust him, but the truth was, he'd only trusted himself all this time. Hell. How did he expect her to move on when he couldn't summon the courage to do it himself? The bombing in Larimer County hadn't been his fault. His team had swept that building. They'd done their job, but the ecoterrorists responsible had been cleverer than he'd estimated. Yet he'd taken on the responsibility for those lives lost when it should've been on those bombers all along.

His determination to live on autopilot, to grit through whatever came his way and isolate himself, had been his way of compartmentalizing, but he didn't want to spend the rest of his life holding on to his own dysfunctional conditioning. He didn't have to do this alone. He didn't want to, and as Macie and Cree progressed through the maze of catastrophe, he realized his life back in Larimer County didn't exist anymore. Because he wasn't the same person he'd been then. Battle Mountain—and the town's highly defensive, most recent recruit for the police department—was his future. And he wasn't going to give up on them. Ever. "Yeah. It's probably a better idea for me to lean on you."

"Gregson! Macie!" Easton Ford's distorted voice filtered through the pops of embers and flames. "Majors! Can anybody hear me?"

Cree dodged a bare nail sticking up from one of the structural beams. His lungs protested against the influx of smoke, and he buried his mouth and nose into his elbow. "In here!"

"Over here!" Macie yelled.

A flashlight beam cut through the smoke and swept across their faces. Pain lightninged through Cree's head at the onslaught, but it gave them a direction through the chaos. In seconds, Easton Ford was tightening an oxygen mask over each of their faces and leading them through the rubble with two firefighters at his back. The building groaned right before the ceiling caved in directly over where they'd been standing. Within a few steps, sunlight swarmed around them. A fire engine skidded to a stop nearby, and a mess of fighters hit the ground. Orders were given and followed, hoses unpacked and emergency personnel in place. Both Macie and Cree were led to a waiting ambulance at the edge of the perimeter, and he couldn't help but scan the officers and rescue trying to get the blaze under control. The entire length of Main Street shops had caught fire, and his stomach pitted. He pulled the mask below his chin. "Where's Alma?"

Easton Ford leveraged his hand against the back of the rig and took a long pull from his own oxygen mask. Confusion rippled across his stoic expression, and the deputy straightened. "She wasn't with you?"

Fear charged through him as Cree memorized every bystander and emergency officer. He shoved off the blanket that had been wrapped around his shoulders and tossed the oxygen mask. Clamping a hand on his dislocated shoulder, he targeted Dr. Chloe Miles speaking with Chief Ford twenty feet away. Alma had left the station to meet with the coroner. If they weren't together... He jogged to catch up to them as the couple parted. "Doc, have you seen Officer Majors? She said she was meeting up with you to reconstruct the victim's skull."

The coroner's eyes widened. "After the explosion, she told me to grab the evidence and get everyone out of the funeral home. I haven't seen her since. She wanted me to keep piecing the skull back together to get an accurate ID on the victim. It's not much, but I was able to scan the portion Alma reassembled."

"You got an ID?" Chief Ford asked.

"It's not a hundred percent match, but it's close. Alma did most of the work going through every piece of bone until a face emerged." She handed off her phone. "Danielle Sawyer. Thirty-four years old, Caucasian female. That's all I've been able to find so far."

Danny. The recipient of the voice mail they recovered from the phone Travis Foster found under his wife's side of the mattress. They had a name, but he couldn't think about that right now. Alma was out here, alone. She needed help.

"Alma wouldn't have just left." He studied the length of shops already threatening to collapse. The killer had called from right outside. If she'd gotten hold of Alma... What blood he had left in his face drained. "She would've... She wouldn't tried to get all these people to safety because no one else was here."

"Chief Ford!" One of the townspeople waved from behind the perimeter tape. Cree wasn't sure of his name or if he'd seen him around town before today. It didn't matter. "That deputy, Officer Majors, she went back into Caffeine and Carbs after pulling Reagan out. I haven't seen her since."

"Damn it." Chief Ford pulled the radio from his belt. "All units, Officer Majors is inside the bakery. I need an EMT and firefighters to help me search the building."

"I'm going with you." Cree stepped into Dr. Miles's personal space. "I need you to reset my shoulder."

"Officer Gregson, you've been through a terrifying trauma." She shook her head. "I think it's best if you—"

"Just do it." He braced for the pain, and Dr. Miles accepted he wasn't going to change his mind. The resulting pop sickened his stomach, and he almost blacked out. Instant relief coiled through him. "Thank you." He took a single step toward the building.

A window exploded from the second story of Caffeine and Carbs, and everybody on the street ducked to protect themselves. Straightening, Cree stared up at what was left of the building just before the supports gave out. Screw his shoulder. He rushed toward the failing structure, but it was too late.

"Cree, no!" Chief Ford latched a hand around his uninjured arm and pulled him back.

The insides of the building gave out first, the outer walls folding soon after. Cree protected his face as ash, fire and brick kicked into the air. Barely able to take a full breath, he waited for the dust to settle. Too long. Squinting through the wall of debris, he nearly tripped over a structural beam. "Alma!"

No. No, no, no, no. Firefighters raced to douse the flames snaking through the rubble, and Cree hauled himself into the pile. Pulling hot bricks and rolling chunks of cement free, he searched every nook and cranny he had access to. "Don't just stand there! Help me!"

Easton Ford, the chief and Dr. Miles each started working through the pile of cement, drywall and framing. The burns along his hands ignited as he tossed another load of bricks over his shoulder. Desperation clawed through him, alive and screaming. They were going to find her. There was no other option. Not for him. "I'm coming, Alma. Just hang on."

Cree hauled the next chunk of rubble free, and a piece of metal glimmered beneath a layer of dust and ash. A police shield. Battle Mountain Police Department. It wouldn't have come detached from her uniform by accident, which meant, Alma had taken it off. Why? The answer solidified in his gut. "She's not here."

Chapter Fourteen

Incessant crying brought her out of darkness.

An infant?

Exhaustion threatened to hold her under, but Alma was stronger. She wiggled her toes in her shoes, then her fingers, bringing herself around limb by limb. Only she couldn't do much more than that. The killer had learned from her mistake this time. Instead of zip ties, ropes encircled Alma's wrists behind her back and her ankles.

"There, there. Mommy's got you. It's going to be okay." That voice. The killer's voice. It drove past the haze of unconsciousness and triggered the mind-numbing fear she never wanted to feel again. A flash of red hair blazed on the other side of the room as her abductor picked up the crying child from a pack-and-play. Recognition flared as Agent Christine Freehan kissed the boy's soft cheek. Travis Foster's son. Pressing her cheek to his, the bomber bounced him in her arms. "She'll be gone soon. I promise. Then it'll just be me and you. Like we wanted from the start."

The side of her face pulsed with her racing heart as Alma took in her surroundings. Old wood creaked as she craned her head back. The small cabin-like home didn't offer much in terms of space. A kitchenette took up one side of the room where she'd been deposited, with a single sofa and the pack-and-play on the other. Bare wood stairs connected the second level to the first, which Alma assumed contained a single bedroom and bathroom.

"Look who's awake." Footsteps reverberated through the floor as Agent Freehan closed in. Pin-straight red hair swayed under the woman's movements. Bangs covered perfectly arched eyebrows and accentuated a long thin nose, and for a fraction of a minute, Alma thought she was staring into the face of the victim she'd found at the base of the gulch. Identical twins. The only difference apart from their hair? The ice in Agent Freehan's gaze. "Just in time."

"You attacked Travis Foster. You kidnapped the baby." Alma didn't understand. The bomber had set out to destroy her sister's identity, tracked her down over years in order to kill her. All so she could have her baby? "Why?"

"I told you why at the lake, Officer Majors." Agent Freehan retraced her steps back to the temporary crib and set the child inside. Crossing into the kitchenette, she wrenched open the refrigerator and pulled a bottle from within. Milk. In as few steps, she handed it off to the boy and soothed his hair as Alma imagined his mother would have. "My sister was the constant favorite while we were growing up. It didn't matter that we were twins, that we shared the same birthday or likes. I was always expendable to our parents. I was always expected to give in to her childish melt-downs to keep the peace or surrender to her every whim."

"Danny." Alma didn't have more than a voice mail as a resource, but based off the stiffness running through the killer's neck and jaw, she'd hit a mark.

Agent Freehan left the boy to feed and straight-ened. "You really are a fine investigator, Officer Ma-jors. It's a shame no one but this pathetic town will ever have the chance to benefit from all that insight."

They were still in Battle Mountain. Although, from the little Alma noted through the single win-dow on the other side of the room, she wasn't sure where or how far out from the city limits they were. "What is this place?"

The bomber exposed her neck as she surveyed the cabin. Shadows lined the tendons running the length of her neck as she slid her hands into her cargo pock-ets. Her leather jacket and bright red T-shirt didn't fit the ATF agent profile at all like she'd imagined, but from what Alma understood, this particular agent didn't really play by the rules. "This place? A safe house of sorts. Well, not a very good one as you can imagine. It didn't work for my sister very long. Danny came across it right after she left her husband

and baby in Ouray. You'd think after so many years on the run, she would've gotten as far from them as possible. Funny thing is, I already knew where she was. I already knew about her husband and the baby. I knew she'd grabbed Mom's cell phone before the fire to call 911. She was smart enough to keep it turned off so I couldn't track her, but a few days ago I got a hit. She'd turned it on. I think now she wanted me to find her. I think she wanted to stop running. So I came to grant her wish."

One step. Two. Agent Freehan refocused on Alma and crouched in front of her. Fingers interlaced, she parted them for a moment, then pressed them back together. "To be honest, she didn't seem all that surprised when she opened the door. More like acceptance. I think she knew then."

Alma worked a broken fingernail against the rope at her back and slowly picked the strands apart. It would take time to get through the whole thing—time she didn't have—but it was worth a shot. Agent Freehan had kidnapped a child to get revenge on her deceased sister. Alma would get him out of here and back home to his father. "Knew what?"

"That I was going to finally get what was owed me." The bomber twisted to check on the baby, still happily plugging away on his bottle. "I worked my entire life to make something of myself, to make our parents proud, and got nothing out of it in return. She glided through life as though everyone owed her. She didn't work for anything, and she didn't deserve what she had."

"The fire that killed your parents all those years ago… You started it." Dryness caught in Alma's throat as she considered the amount of hatred and rage it would've taken to murder the very people who'd raised you.

"Once I got to be in high school, I realized I wasn't ever going to make a difference in how my parents saw me." Agent Freehan shoved to her feet, unholstering the weapon she'd taken from Alma. She hit the magazine release and caught the heavy metal before it dropped to the floor. Thumbing each bullet free, she let the rounds scatter around her boots. "I wasted years trying to impress them. Straight A's all through middle school and high school, sports, early college courses. None of it mattered, and when I asked my mother why she loved Danny more than she loved me? She told me I didn't need the attention, that I could take care of myself. Turns out, she was right. So I did exactly that. I took care of myself, and I haven't looked back."

"You killed them because they favored your sister over you?" One of the bullets rolled against Alma's shoe, and she set her boot over it as slowly as possible so as not to draw attention. "And what about the bombing at Galaxy Electronics or the police station? Did you do those because your parents didn't love you enough?"

"I couldn't very well have you tracing the devices back to me through the components I stole from that dilapidated store, now, could I? The government trained me better than that." Agent Freehan cocked her head to one side. "As for the police station, I needed to make sure the evidence Silverton's bomb squad collected from the scene was destroyed. Can't have anything threatening my job with the ATF. How else will I support this little one myself?"

A smile partnered with Alma's humorless laugh. All this time, she'd convinced herself the killer they were after had been one step ahead. Turned out, she was just as human as the rest of them. "Well, there was your first mistake."

Amusement bled from Agent Freehan's expression, and the bomber peeled her hands from inside her pockets. "What was that?"

"The coroner took custody of your sister's remains from the gulch." Alma slid the bullet under her shoe another inch closer to her hands.

"I realize this might be your first homicide investigation, Officer Majors, but believe it or not, that's protocol," Freehan said. "That's exactly what I was counting on."

"But you haven't done your homework." She felt the tip of the bullet brush against her fingers, and she pinned it between both hands. The bullet itself wouldn't do a damn bit of good without her weapon, but once she unscrewed the tip from the casing, the edge might be sharp enough to cut through the rope. "You see, after the mining companies pulled out of town and took all their money with them, there wasn't enough resources to establish a medical examiner's office. The closest ME we have is over in Grand Junction." She twisted the tip of the bullet free, catching it before it hit the floor and gave away her plan. "That said, Chief Ford could appoint a coroner. Dr. Miles is great at her job and is able to conduct autopsies, but she doesn't have a lab. And her office isn't anywhere near the police station."

Seconds distorted into a minute, into what felt like an hour.

"I know what you're trying to do, Officer Majors. If I hadn't already checked you for a wire, I'd seriously question why you're dragging this out. But from the way you've been hiding your hands from me, I'm guessing you're working on your binds." Agent Freehan tossed Alma's weapon to the far side of the room. "Maybe it's time to end this once and for all."

The rope strands unwound, and faster than she expected, Alma's hands broke free. "I think you're right." Hauling her feet forward, she swept the killer's legs out from under her.

Agent Freehan hit the ground. Her head snapped back, and the killer's eyes widened slightly.

Alma didn't wait for her to recover. She slapped one hand over the agent's ankle and pulled the blade holstered beneath her cargo pants. In a clean swipe, she severed the ropes around her ankles and shoved to stand. She lunged toward the pack-and-play to grab the baby. Too slow. The pain in her shoulder flared as the bomber dug strong fingers into the hole the victim's bone had left behind. A scream escaped her control, and Alma doubled over to grit through it.

"Let me make one thing clear, Officer Majors." Agent Freehand circled into Alma's vision and gripped her by the back of the neck. "You don't get to touch my son."

The stitches in her side stretched with each over-exaggerated inhale. "He's not your son. He never will be, and I'm going to take him home." Alma kicked out as hard as she could. Her heel connected with Agent Freehan's knee, but not enough to shatter bone. The killer launched a fist straight into Alma's temple, and Alma staggered back into a faux plant beside the kitchenette.

"He is home." Agent Freehan charged.

CREE SWIPED FIRE hose water from his face.

The edges of Alma's shield cut into his palm as he took in what was left of the shops along Main Street, including the station. He pressed his free hand into his ribs. One broken. Maybe two. He'd been lucky the damn injury hadn't punctured his lungs. Considering the circumstances, he and Macie were both lucky to walk out of that station alive.

The town wasn't lucky enough.

Tears, sobs and disbelief filtered through the crowds pressing against the perimeter. Easton had gone through for statements as fire and rescue fought to get the blaze from spreading to any other buildings. No one had seen Alma after she'd gone back into the bakery for another bystander. But there had been reports of a midsize sedan leaving the scene a few minutes before EMTs found the baker's assistant behind the building with minor smoke inhalation. No one had been in a calm enough state to catch a plate number while their town burned around them, but Cree's gut told him Alma had been in that car. Now all he had to do was find her.

Rock and wood sizzled under the influence of hose water. While the flames had retreated for the time being, fire and rescue would ensure the blaze was completely neutralized before letting anyone close. He didn't need to get close. He needed a lead. Rivers of water and ash squished under his feet. He could still feel the heat emanating from what was left of Caffeine and Carbs. The burn lanced across the damage already done to his hands and neck from the bomb rigged to his truck. The dragon had done its job here, consuming some of these people's livelihoods along with it. He wiped a trail of sweat from the back of his neck as he studied every inch of the ground behind the line of shops. And stopped.

Tire tracks. Headed east. Too close together to

belong to an SUV or pickup. The sedan that witnesses had noticed fleeing the scene? Cree shoved to his feet.

"You got something?" Chief Ford swept dark eyes along the backside of the row of shops.

"A few people behind the tape described a late-model sedan driving away from the scene. These are a match for size." He nodded to the tracks giving way under the onslaught of fire hose water. "You're going to want to get a cast of these as soon as possible. No telling how much longer fire and rescue is going to soak this area." Cree walked along the treads left behind in the dirt. His truck had been totaled with that third bomb. He needed a vehicle. "I'm going after Alma."

"Gregson." Ford tossed him a set of keys just as Cree turned to face him. "Bring her back home alive. You got me? Whatever it takes."

"I give you my word, Chief." Cree nodded. Curling his fingers around the keys, he slipped through the break between buildings and headed for the pickup truck parked across the street in front of Hopper's Hardware.

The truck started with the easiest of provocation from the ignition, and the mobile data terminal mounted between the front seats flickered to life. He planted Alma's badge on the dashboard. Lucky for him, the department's central computer wasn't located inside the station. Instead, the system connected wirelessly to Colorado's Bureau of Investigation. He twisted to type the victim's name and hit enter. Danielle Sawyer. Her photo filled the screen, a perfect match to the missing person report Travis Foster had filed for his wife. Dr. Miles had been right. Alma had found the victim's identity.

The computer ticked as it processed his request for Agent Christine Freehan's background information. Another photo filled the screen, almost identical to the first. Same birthday listed as for Danielle. Twins?

He searched for properties in Danielle Sawyer's name but came up empty.

No. She wouldn't have used her own name on a home deed. Not if she'd gone to such lengths to change her identity on the run. She would've used what was available. No connection to Danielle Sawyer. If she'd listened to that voice mail from her sister, it would've triggered her flight instinct. Maybe enough for her to consider leaving her family behind to keep them safe from her past. "In that case…"

Cree searched for foreclosed or abandoned properties. Danielle Sawyer had been killed here in Battle Mountain. Stood to reason she'd been hiding here when the bomber had finally caught up with her. The MDT spat out a list. He ran through it, one by one. The victim had been on the run since high school. She'd known what she was doing. Problem was, whoever had hunted her all these years was better. Nothing too close to town. Would've made it hard for Danielle Sawyer to stay under the radar, but not too far, either. She would've wanted access to a vehicle if she'd needed to ditch hers and groceries if she intended to stay a while. "Where did your sister find you?"

A cabin crept up the screen, and Cree stopped scrolling. Familiarity lanced through him. He pressed back into the leather seat. His grandfather's cabin. It had been years since the old man had passed away, and Cree hadn't ever intended to go back. Hadn't hired anyone to take care of it while he was on tour or working the bomb squad up in Larimer County.

It was the perfect safe house.

Not too far.

Not too close.

And nowhere near any nosy neighbors.

"Gotcha." Cree shut the terminal lid and put the truck into gear. Tires protested as he hit the accelerator and pulled away from the curb. The steering wheel caught on the blisters under his fingers. Sunlight reflected off the ash-covered badge he'd set on the dashboard, keeping him in the moment. Trees thickened the faster he raced along one of two roads out of town until he couldn't see Battle Mountain in the rearview mirror at all.

His sense of direction and the fact his grandfather had forced him to memorize a map of the area had him pulling off the main road earlier than what would get him to the cabin fastest. The truck's hood dipped and rose along the dirt and gravel road, and he slowed to a near crawl so as not to kick up dust. If the bomber had ambushed her sister at the cabin and then gone to extreme lengths to hide her involvement, she might not have had time to get the lay of the land. He cut the truck's automatic daytime lights and pulled in headfirst beneath an overgrown tree Cree had used for target practice all those years ago. "Here we go."

Eyes on the cabin higher up the mountain, he reached for the glove box and found another of the chief's backup weapons. He shouldered out of the truck and closed the driver's-side door behind him as quietly as possible. After checking the magazine, he loaded a round into the chamber and wedged it between his lower back and waistband. He rounded the hood of the truck. Hatchet scars scored the thin bark along the tree's trunk, and at the base, covered in pine needles, he found the hatchet his grandfather had gifted him for his eighteenth birthday, the last time they'd been together before the old man had passed. Cree smoothed his thumb along the handle, then gripped it hard.

He kept low and moved fast through the trees, making sure he was never in sight of the cabin's west window positioned in the living room. His heart thudded steadily behind his ears. A late-model gray sedan demanded attention from the gravel driveway, and confirmation pulsed through him. Crouching low behind the vehicle, he slid his fingers the length of the tire treads. Same pattern he'd discovered behind the bakery where Alma had last been seen. This was it. His partner was in there, and he wasn't going back to town without her.

The muscles along the backs of his legs burned as he maneuvered around the rear of the vehicle. Distraction. Agent Freehan had trained with the best of the best over the years. She knew her way around explosive devices. No telling how many she'd planted in case someone got too close.

There. The stockpile of wood had grown since the time he'd left this place behind. Whether it'd been seen to by Danielle Sawyer or her sister in recent months, it didn't matter. What did matter was the white bricks of C4 hidden inside. Travis Foster's construction manager had reported twenty pounds of the explosive missing from their worksite. The bomber had already gone through at least ten between the gulch, Galaxy Electronics, Cree's truck, the lake, and the station, leaving ten pounds unaccounted for. Agent Freehan had mostly likely positioned similar devices around the perimeter here.

Cree gripped the hatchet before embedding it into a nearby log. Crossing beneath the west window, he crouched in front of the stockpile and pulled the device free. No countdown. This one had been set up to detonate with a remote trigger. A cell phone in this case. Clever. One press of a button and the entire cabin and the surrounding property would go up in flames. Carefully detaching the cell phone from the device, he scanned through the call log. Only one number in the history. Memorizing it, he reattached the phone and worked his way back to the vehicle in the driveway. He slid under the frame and used the pliability of the C4 to attach the homemade device to the undercarriage. "Let's see what you do with a taste of your own medicine, Freehan."

In seconds, he left the safety of the vehicle and retreated into the woods, finding five more devices like the one he'd discovered positioned strategically at the cabin's structural walls. Taking position at the clearing's edge, he unpocketed his own phone and dialed the number from the trigger's call history. The line rang once. Twice.

"Agent Freehan." The same voice he'd heard over Danielle Sawyer's voice mail grated along his nerves, out of breath, and Cree's body tightened in response. The screams of a kid staticked through the line, and his insides constricted.

"Let my partner walk out of there on her own two feet with the boy, and I'll let you do the same," he said.

"Officer Gregson, how nice of you to join us. I'm curious, though. How did you get this number? Couldn't have been from the friend you had looking into me at the ATF. You and I both know I've been doing this too long to make a simple mistake like using my work phone for personal calls." Freehan's outline crossed in front of the east window as she searched the perimeter. She wanted him to know she knew he'd sent someone to look into her, throw him off guard, maybe make him rethink his approach, but it wouldn't work. Red hair swept over her shoulders as she leaned into the glass, and he backed into the tree line. She moved onto the next window, making it easy to track her movements. "You took apart my security system, didn't you?"

"Not all of it. Just enough to ensure whatever you had planned won't work." Cree kept to the trees as he rounded the property. "Where are Alma and the boy?"

"Right here, of course," Freehan said. "Although I can't guarantee your partner will be here much longer."

"We'll see about that." He ended the call, then dialed a second number. Cree crossed the overgrown space between the tree line and the south wall of the cabin. He hit the green button to connect.

The explosion ripped through the sedan.

Chapter Fifteen

The boy's screams kept her conscious, almost willing her to stay in the fight.

Then an explosion rocked through one side of the cabin.

The quake rolled beneath her and threatened to bring down the entire structure. The window above the kitchenette shattered. Glass rained down around her. Alma rolled to her bleeding side. Her stitches hadn't been enough to keep her wound together during the fight, but she couldn't give in. Not yet. Blood escaped from between her clenched teeth. She spat to clear her mouth and her senses as Agent Freehan rocked back on her heels.

Now was her chance.

Alma wiped the blood from her mouth and lunged.

Shoving the bomber over the countertop, she gripped the back of Freehan's head and rocketed it into the counter. One of the drawers shook from the impact. Alma fisted a handful of the agent's long hair but had to let go at the swift swipe of a knife from the butcher block. She fell back against the floor as Agent Freehan advanced.

"Nobody is taking him from me." The baby's cries intensified as if on cue. Both hands wrapped around the knife's handle, the bomber held it over her head. Ready to plunge it in Alma's chest.

Alma rolled as fast as she could just as the tip of the blade imbedded into the floor, and she got to her feet. Spanning her arms wide, she searched for a weapon—anything that would counter a kitchen knife—and brushed against a set of dusty curtains. She ripped one panel free just as Agent Freehan attacked, knife first.

Alma wrapped the fabric around the bomber's wrist and twisted as hard as she could. The pop of a fractured bone barely registered through the toddler's screams. She pinned her attacker's arm against her injured side and tightened her hold on the curtain panel. "Your sister didn't deserve to die in that gulch. All she wanted was to escape the past, but you wouldn't let her. You were so determined to make her pay for something she wasn't responsible for that you wasted your entire life instead of trying to move on."

An echo of that pain reverberated through Alma as she considered how many months she'd wasted following the same path. Hurt, determined to be alone, using the past as a crutch to keep herself from moving forward. But Cree had brought hope and light into her life. He'd given her the strength to face down the shadows that had become so deeply ingrained she hadn't seen a way out of the darkness. That strength, she realized, had been there all along. It had just taken someone like him to prove she was more than a victim, more than a trauma survivor. That she wasn't alone. "You're going to spend the rest of your life behind bars because you wouldn't take responsibility for your own happiness."

Agent Freehan launched her free arm for another strike, but Alma was faster. With both hands pinned, the killer raged to gain some semblance of control. "You have no idea what she took from me."

"She didn't take anything." Alma hauled her boot into the side of the bomber's knee, and the agent collapsed to the floor. Tightening her hold around the curtain panel, she forced Agent Freehan to drop the knife. Metal met wood with a hard thud. "You were never a victim. No matter how many times you've tried to convince yourself otherwise, you don't get to have your happily-ever-after." The bomber's own words from the voice mail she'd left her sister echoed through Alma's head. "It's over."

"No." Agent Freehan struggled against the pressure on her broken wrist, a fire Alma had seen all too often during her marriage in the killer's eyes. "This isn't over. This isn't how it ends for me."

The boy quieted down, watching in angst, but still clenching small fists, his bottle forgotten. The cabin's front door crashed inward, and Alma's fight instincts automatically responded. Until recognition flared. "Cree."

Her partner stood in the doorframe, what looked like a hatchet in one hand and his phone in the other. He scanned the room and took in her hold on Agent Freehan. Cree had come for her. "Looks like I missed one hell of a party. Agent Freehan, nice to meet you face-to-face."

The bomber didn't answer, didn't even seem to breathe as she seethed.

A wave of dizziness crowded Alma's head as the entire investigation over the past four days led to this. She released her numb grip from the curtain panel and slumped back against the wall. She forced her fingernails into the palms of her hands to keep herself from mentally detaching. The boy's cries filtered in and out through the pulse thudding hard at the back of her skull, and she crossed the room. Red stains of distress across the baby's face paled as she reached into the pack-and-play and hefted him to her chest. "You're safe now. I'm going to get you to your daddy at the hospital. Okay? He's worried about you, but you'll be together soon enough. You're safe." She automatically bounced him on her hip, pressing a hand into his back. The cries quieted, and she set her temple against his warm cheek.

"Any sudden movements, Agent Freehan, and your car will be the least of your worries." Cree wrenched the killer's hands behind her back, ignoring the groan of pain from her broken wrist, and produced a set of cuffs from his back pocket.

Sirens echoed off the cliffs, and Alma stepped near the window in time to see a Battle Mountain patrol cruiser dipping and climbing up the dirt road. Flames charred stretches of gravel as she took in the aftermath but didn't shift toward the cabin.

It was over.

She soothed small circles into the boy's back as Cree led Agent Freehan toward the front door. Then froze. The curtain panel stretched the length of the floor where she'd left it. But where was the knife she'd forced the killer to drop? Alma turned after Cree. Too late. "Watch out!"

Agent Freehan wrenched free of Cree's hold and dropped to the floor. Faster than Alma thought possible, the bomber rolled, maneuvering her cuffed wrists under her boots, just as Alma had at the lake. Freehan pulled the knife from beneath her leather jacket and focused her wrath at Alma.

One second. Two.

"No!" Alma spun to protect the boy and braced for the striking pain of the blade.

Only it never came.

A rough exhale reached her ears. She twisted around, her hold tight on the boy. And found Cree standing between her and Agent Freehand. Too close. The woman's expression warped from surprise into satisfaction, and Alma's heart shot into her throat. Just as the front door burst open. "Cree?"

He didn't answer.

"Battle Mountain PD! On the ground! Now!" Easton Ford raised his weapon and targeted Agent Freehan.

The killer raised both hands still bound by the cuffs and backed away from Cree, the knife no longer in her grip. She followed instructions and got down on one knee, then the other, before laying face-first on the floor. Cold eyes found Alma, and Agent Freehan smirked. "You took something of mine. I take something of yours."

Cree collapsed, drawing a panicked scream from her throat.

"No!" Tightening her hold on the toddler, Alma dropped to her knees as the pain in her shoulder screamed for relief. It took more effort than she'd imagined to turn him onto his back. A line of blood escaped the corner of his mouth. "Hang on. Help is already on the way. Just hang on."

Forest green eyes found hers—slowly—and Cree intertwined his hand with hers. The wound spat blood around the blade still protruding from his rib cage. Too deep, but she couldn't risk removing it. He might bleed internally before the EMTs had a chance. "Your...theory worked. The skull. You...found her."

"Shh. Try not to talk right now." In an instant, she was back in that gulch, watching an innocent life drain in front of her eyes, and there hadn't been anything she could do. "Save your energy."

"Danielle Sawyer." A rough cough clenched every muscle in his body, and Alma strengthened her grip in his hand. "You found her."

Tears burned in her eyes. Tears for the pain he suffered, for the time she'd wasted trying to hide from the world, for the potential loss between them. Tears for the victim and the pain she must've endured to protect her son. The boy set his head against her shoulder. Her side protested from the added weight of his small body, but she wasn't going to let him go. "We found her. Together."

Easton dragged Agent Freehan outside.

Cree's eyelids fell as he sucked in a ragged breath. His grip on her hand lightened, but Alma would hold on longer for the both of them if that was what she was required to do. "I was never…going to go back."

"I know." Distant sirens bounced off the cliff walls and pierced through the pops of the smoldering vehicle outside. Her knees went numb pressed against the floor, but she wouldn't leave him. Ever. Cree had saved her. In more ways than one.

Without his knowledge of explosives and all the packages they came in, Agent Freehan would've gotten her way days ago. And without his compassion and ability to see past the mask she wore for the people of this town, she wouldn't have developed the strength to rise above her hurt. Therapy, a ground-breaking book, a new mind set on life and recovery—none of it had compared to his willingness to help her to be seen again instead of hiding behind the pain. She wasn't a lone survivor. He'd made her story part of his story, and she loved him for it. Alma soothed circles into his hand just as he'd done for her back at his apartment. She had to keep him talking. She had to keep him alive. "Cree, look at me."

The seconds ticked off one by one, and the pressure behind her rib cage intensified the longer he lay there, unmoving.

His eyelids strained to open, and a hint of a smile tugged at one corner of his mouth. The sirens were growing closer, but Cree was fighting a losing battle. They wouldn't make it in time. "Hey, partner."

She shifted on her knees, centering herself and the toddler in his limited vision. Her tears dropped to his T-shirt. "I love you."

"You certainly know how to party down here in the middle of nowhere," a deep voice said.

A sense of familiarity punctuated through the weight of painkillers and gravity cementing Cree in place. He knew that voice. Although it had been a couple days since he'd heard it last. Prying his eyes open, he took in the whitewashed walls he'd hoped never to see again. Same monitors, too. He took in the sterile tile and scratchy bedding. Battle Mountain's emergency clinic.

Movement registered off to his left from the side of the bed, and the outline of well-built strength consumed his attention. Kendric Hudson locked mishappen brown eyes on him, and the past rushed to meet the present. The ATF's newest bomb squad technician instructor Cree had pulled from the ecoterrorist attack had sustained permanent scarring along one side of his face. The same scarring carved down Cree's back.

"You look as bad as I feel." His voice scraped along his throat as Cree attempted to sit higher in the bed. A dull ache ignited across his midsection. Two broken ribs were nothing compared to cold metal slicing through body parts never meant to see the light of day. A groan escaped his control, and he set his head back against the pillows stacked behind him. "The sheriff called in a favor, didn't he? He sent you to convince me to come back."

It wasn't a question. While the ATF had to absorb the consequences of letting one of their investigators off her leash and had most likely sent a few of their own to run damage control, Kendric hadn't gone back into the field since the bombing in Loveland. He trained the new recruits to save their own lives after barely escaping the bombing that had given him those scars.

His former teammate scratched at one corner of his mouth. "I think my face is supposed to be some kind of guilt trip, a reminder of all the good you've done in the past. Then again, I'm pretty sure your own scars do the trick." The tech's leather vest folded in on itself as soft as poured chocolate as Kendric took a seat. He motioned to something across the room, and Cree caught sight of Alma curled up on her side on the window seat, asleep. "Was it worth it?"

Cree tried to clear the emotion from his throat. She was safe, alive. Thirty seconds. If he'd been thirty seconds later, he would've lost her all over again. Snippets of their last conversation broke through his exhaustion and ignited the pain in his side. Even after she'd severed ties between them, he hadn't had a choice. Putting himself between Agent Freehan and Alma had been instinct, a last-ditch effort to prove their partnership had changed him, that they worked better as a team. Although he could've done without the blade shoved in his gut to make his point. "How... How long has she been here?"

"Since you landed your sorry butt here in the first place." Kendric's voice softened as though he were trying to keep himself from waking the reserve officer Cree had fallen head over heels for. "From what I hear, you're a damn hero. You made it possible for her and that baby to walk out of there and exposed a corrupt ATF agent in the process. The sheriff and the mayor's office are already taking credit, claiming they're the ones who sent you down here undercover to find the truth. Bastards."

Cree studied the slow rise and fall of Alma's shoulders, lost in her instead of what Kendric had said. He'd escaped Loveland to hide from the pain of failing the innocent lives he'd tried to save before the attack, and now, one of the men caught in the blast was here. Two separate lives in the same room. One before he'd come to Battle Mountain. One after. In reality, they weren't separate at all. Mere pieces of a whole. Just as the time he'd grown up living off the land his grandfather owned and his service in the military. Each life had built on the next, leading to this one, preparing him for her. Alma. "Thanks for your help on this case." He rolled his head into the pillows to face his teammate. "I owe you."

"More than tackling me to the ground when that bomb went off and taking the brunt of the blast?" Kendric shook his head. "You still don't get it, do you, man? I know why you left, same as you know why I applied to the ATF. You've been blaming yourself for what happened, but I don't show off these scars because you couldn't get me free of that blast. I show them off because I'm alive to do it." His teammate stood as Alma swept her uninjured forearm over her eyes in the window seat. "Now get over yourself and get back to living your life. Wherever you need to do it." Kendric headed for the door. "I'll tell the sheriff to go jump off a bridge for you."

A laugh rumbled through Cree's chest, and he wrapped both arms around his midsection, short of breath. "My answer is yes, by the way," Cree said. "To your question before. It was worth it."

Kendric paused at the door, his gaze on Alma. "Then, by all means, don't let me or anyone else stand in your way."

"You should stick around." Cree held his breath as his partner stirred. "This town has a way of making sure those wounds we like to pretend don't exist won't scar."

"Maybe I will." Kendric opened the door to make his escape. "See you around, Gregson."

The door clicked closed behind him.

Alma sighed from the window seat, slowly pushing herself upright. Sweeping her hair out of her face, she squinted into the fluorescent lights overhead. "Oh, sorry about that. I just meant to close my eyes for a few minutes. Was that Agent Hudson I heard?"

"You two know each other?" Warmth that had nothing to do with the painkillers flooded through him as he memorized her voice all over again.

"We talked a little in the hall when I ran out to fill your water mug." She pressed her palm into the hollow of her eye and stifled a yawn. "He's been coordinating with ATF to transfer Agent Freehan back to Washington, DC. They're going to prosecute her in federal court for using bureau resources for personal use, attempted murder on law enforcement officials, kidnapping, and the murder of her sister. All in all, she's looking at a life sentence."

"Wow." Cree tipped his head back, brushing the pillows. "What else did I miss? What happened with the baby?"

"He's good. We got him checked out as soon the EMTs got you to the hospital. Completely healthy. Seems Agent Freehan hadn't abducted him to get back at her sister as we thought. I think she just wanted a piece of that happiness Danielle Sawyer found inside her own little family. Even knowing that boy could never really be hers." Alma brought one arm up to fold against her midsection but thought better of it. "Last I checked, Travis Foster was downstairs waiting for the on-call doctor to discharge them. After everything that happened, Ouray Police now believe Erica was asking for a restraining order to protect Travis and the baby. Not get away from them. With Agent Freehan under arrest, they're safe. They can go home and grieve. Thanks to you."

"And you?" He motioned to her side where she seemed to be holding herself unconsciously. "How's the side?"

"I may have torn a few stitches during the fight. Nothing that couldn't be restitched." She sucked in a deep breath. "Overall, I'm glad it's over. For my first response call, I'd give it a two out of five stars."

"Just two?" he asked. "Come on. There were explosions, high-speed chases, a rogue agent, an abducted child and romance. Any action movie fan would've at least given it three stars."

"Romance?" She narrowed her gaze, amusement tugging at her mouth. "And where in this investigation was there time for a romance?"

Cree reached out, walking his fingers along her lower back, and pulled her closer to the bed. "Right now." He smiled as she leaned in to press her mouth to his, and the pain through his side dwindled to a dull awareness. The power she held over him hadn't forced him to make careless decisions or act against his instincts. No. Instead, she'd showed him the real meaning of strength by standing as an example of dedication, justice and forgiveness.

She pulled back and motioned to his side. "How's the wound?"

"Medium-rare. Thanks for asking." He shifted in the bed. Didn't help.

"Macie told me what happened at the police station." She directed her gaze to his hand as she interlaced her fingers with his, just as she had in the cabin. "I was so mad with myself after our last conversation, I'd turned off my radio. I'm sorry I wasn't there. I'm sorry I—"

"You don't need to apologize to me, Alma. Not for looking out for yourself." He soothed small circles in the space between her index finger and thumb. "You've been through a lot these past few years. Something no one should ever have to face. You and I both know the longer we take to confront the pain, the harder it will be to move on."

"I thought I had," she said. "Moved on. I came home to Battle Mountain. I signed on as a reserve officer. I didn't even have the bruises anymore. I thought I was free from having to feel that pain ever again." Her shoulders shook as she tried to hold back the sorrow building in her voice. "Then you pulled me out of the lake after Agent Freehan tried to kill me, and I got scared. I started having these feelings for you, just as I'd had feelings for my ex all those years ago, and I didn't want to… I didn't want to let down my guard again when I didn't know what was on the other side. That's why I told you to go back to Loveland."

Cree didn't know what to say to that, what to think.

"I've lived with this empty space in my chest since the divorce was final, like a part of me stayed behind." She squeezed his hand. "But when I saw the aftermath of the bombing at the police station, and I realized it'd been filled. By you. I didn't want to lose that. I didn't feel alone anymore, and I didn't want you to try to salvage your former life." Her shoulders deflated as though she'd finally let go of the weight of the world. "I don't know what the future holds or what your plans are, but for the first time, I think I'm okay with that. As long as we're together, there isn't anything that will scare me more than knowing I almost lost you. Because I love you."

"I love you, too." Pure excitement lanced through

him as Cree strained to pull her in for another kiss. She met him halfway, and the guilt, the shame and embarrassment—none of it had changed a damn thing. It had never served him other than to keep him from letting it all go. There wasn't any room left for the past to come between them. What that meant in regards to his career, he didn't know. But his life would be here. In Battle Mountain. With Alma. For however long she'd tolerate him. "It's going to be harder to escape the clinic this time, but I'll give it my best shot, Officer Majors."

She hit him with that gut-wrenching smile. "I'll grab the Jell-O."

Epilogue

Battle Mountain was on fire.

Kendric Hudson surveyed the destruction over-taking the small town's Main Street as he drove through. Fire and rescue had smothered the flames, but the slushy, acrid scent of smoke and the devasta-tion in the residents' expressions couldn't be washed clean. The people here had lost everything.

He knew the feeling.

A pair of firefighters hauled cinder blocks from the rubble and tossed them into a backhoe a few feet away. The hard thunk of rock meeting metal rang loud despite the cocoon created by the cab of his truck. It would take months for crews to get through this mess, and what were the people of this town sup-posed to do until then? Not only had they lost part of their town to one of the very agents they'd trusted to do right by her duty, but they'd nearly lost their homes to the fire Agent Christine Freehan had set west of city limits.

Battle Mountain PD didn't have the resources or

the manpower to assure the stricken faces catching his eye. They barely had enough reserve officers to keep their heads above water.

A panicked holler breached through the driver's-side window a split second before the walls of one of the burned-out buildings crumbled. A firefighter standing nearby twisted around, staring up at the oncoming debris. Only he wasn't fast enough. The wall buried him faster than it had taken Kendric to slam on the brakes. He threw the truck in Park, then pumped his legs as fast as they would carry him to help. Two more emergency personnel closed in on either side of them. "Over here!"

Wood disintegrated in his hands as he chucked rock, damaged beams and cement to the side. In minutes, he caught sight of a single hand reaching toward the surface. Clasping the man's grip to let the firefighter know they were there, Kendric worked with one hand to dislodge him from the debris. Soon, they'd moved enough rubble to get him to the surface. Blood streaked down the man's face beneath the cracked shield of his gear. "We've got you, buddy. It's going to be okay."

He handed the firefighter off to his crew. EMTs ran to meet them, but Kendric couldn't move. Swiping the sweat from his forehead with the back of his ash-covered hand, he fell back into the rubble to catch his breath. Hell. He hadn't had this much excitement since a wall of flames had consumed Cree Gregson's body during their last assignment together.

His former teammate's words echoed through his head. *This town has a way of making sure those wounds we like to pretend don't exist won't scar.* He had no idea what the hell that meant or what wounds Cree thought he was pretending didn't exist.

But maybe he could stick around long enough to find out.

* * * * *

 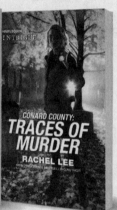

#2103 CONARD COUNTY: CHRISTMAS CRIME SPREE
Conard County: The Next Generation • by Rachel Lee

Savage attacks on several women in parson Molly Canton's parish threaten the holiday season. Assisting Detective Callum McCloud's investigation, Molly is drawn to the tortured man. But once the detective realizes these attacks are a smoke screen obscuring the real target—Molly—the stakes escalate...especially now that Molly's goodness has breached Callum's calloused heart.

#2104 POLICE DOG PROCEDURAL
K-9s on Patrol • by Lena Diaz

When police lieutenant Macon Ridley and his K-9, Bogie, respond to a call from Daniels Canine Academy, they discover a baby on DCA's doorstep. Even more surprising, the chemistry that sizzled when Macon first met Emma Daniels sparks once again. Now, not only is an innocent infant's life at stake but so is Emma's...

#2105 EAGLE MOUNTAIN CLIFFHANGER
Eagle Mountain Search and Rescue • by Cindi Myers

Responding to the reports of a car accident, newcomer Deputy Jake Gwynn finds a murder scene instead. Search and rescue paramedic Hannah Richards tried to care for the likely suspect before he slipped away—and now he's gone from injured man to serial killer on the loose. And she's his next target.

#2106 SMALL TOWN VANISHING
Covert Cowboy Soldiers • by Nicole Helm

Rancher Brody Thompson's got a knack for finding things, even in the wild and remote Wyoming landscape he's just begun to call home. So when Kate Phillips asks for Brody's help in solving her father's decade-old disappearance, he's intrigued. But there's a steep price to pay for uncovering the truth...

#2107 PRESUMED DEAD
Defenders of Battle Mountain • by Nichole Severn

Forced to partner up, reserve officer Kendric Hudson and missing persons agent Campbell Dwyer work a baffling abduction case that gets more dangerous with each new revelation. As they battle a mounting threat, they must also trust one another with their deepest secrets.

#2108 WYOMING WINTER RESCUE
Cowboy State Lawmen • by Juno Rushdan

Trying to stop a murderous patient has consumed psychotherapist Lynn Delgado. But when a serial killer targets Lynn, she must accept protection and turn to lawman Nash Garner for help. As she flees the killer in a raging blizzard, Nash follows, risking everything to save the woman he's falling for.

The whole desperate plan began simply as a last-ditch attempt to save his life. He never intended for anyone to get hurt. That day, not long after Thanksgiving, he walked into the bank full of hope. It was the first time he'd ever asked for a loan. It was also the first time he'd ever seen executive loan officer Carla Richmond.

When he tapped at her open doorway, she looked up from that big desk of hers. He thought she was too young and pretty with her big blue eyes and all that curly chestnut-brown hair to make the decision as to whether he lived or died.

She had a great smile as she got to her feet to offer him a seat.

He felt so out of place in her plush office that he stood in the doorway nervously kneading the brim of his worn baseball cap for a moment before stepping in. As he did, her blue-eyed gaze took in his ill-fitting clothing hanging on his rangy body, his bad haircut, his large, weathered hands.

He told himself that she'd already made up her mind before he even sat down. She didn't give men like him a second look—let alone money. Like his father always said, bankers never gave dough to poor people who actually needed it. They just helped their rich friends.

Right away Carla Richmond made him feel small with her questions about his employment record, what he had for collateral, why he needed the money and how he planned to repay it. He'd recently lost one crappy job and was in the process of starting another temporary one, and all he had to show for the years he'd worked hard labor since high school was an old pickup and a pile of bills.

He took the forms she handed him and thanked her, knowing he wasn't going to bother filling them in. On the way out of her office, he balled them up and dropped them in the trash. All the way to his pickup, he mentally kicked himself for being such a fool. What had he expected?

No one was going to give him money, even to save his life—especially some woman in a suit behind a big desk in an air-conditioned office. It didn't matter that she didn't have a clue how desperate he really was. All she'd seen when she'd looked at him was a loser. To think that he'd bought a new pair of jeans with the last of his cash and borrowed a too-large button-up shirt from a former coworker for this meeting.

After climbing into his truck, he sat for a moment, too scared and sick at heart to start the engine. The worst part was the thought of going home and telling Jesse. The way his luck was going, she would walk out on him. Not that he could blame her, since his gambling had gotten them into this mess.

He thought about blowing off work, since his new job was only temporary anyway, and going straight to the bar. Then he reminded himself that he'd spent the last of his money on the jeans. He couldn't even afford a beer. His own fault, he reminded himself. He'd only made things worse when he'd gone to a loan shark for cash and then stupidly gambled the money, thinking he could make back what he owed and then some when he won. He'd been so sure his luck had changed for the better when he'd met Jesse.

Last time the two thugs had come to collect the interest on the loan, they'd left him bleeding in the dirt outside his rented house. They would be back any day.

With a curse, he started the pickup. A cloud of exhaust blew out the back as he headed home to face Jesse with the bad news. Asking for a loan had been a long shot, but still he couldn't help thinking about the disappointment he'd see in her eyes when he told her. They'd planned to go out tonight for an expensive dinner with the loan money to celebrate.

As he drove home, his humiliation began to fester like a sore that just wouldn't heal. Had he known even then how this was going to end? Or was he still telling himself he was just a nice guy who'd made some mistakes, had some bad luck and gotten involved with the wrong people?

Don't miss
Christmas Ransom *by B.J. Daniels,*
available December 2022 wherever
Harlequin books and ebooks are sold.

Harlequin.com

HIEXP0922

Get 4 FREE REWARDS!

We'll send you 2 FREE Books plus 2 FREE Mystery Gifts.

FREE
Value Over
$20

Both the **Harlequin Intrigue®** and **Harlequin® Romantic Suspense** series feature compelling novels filled with heart-racing action-packed romance that will keep you on the edge of your seat.

HARLEQUIN
PLUS

Announcing a **BRAND-NEW** multimedia subscription service for romance fans like you!

Read, Watch and Play.

Experience the easiest way to get the romance content you crave.

Start your **FREE 7 DAY TRIAL** at www.harlequinplus.com/freetrial.

Love Harlequin romance?

DISCOVER.

Be the first to find out about promotions, news and exclusive content!

f Facebook.com/HarlequinBooks

🐦 Twitter.com/HarlequinBooks

📷 Instagram.com/HarlequinBooks

P Pinterest.com/HarlequinBooks

You Tube YouTube.com/HarlequinBooks

ReaderService.com

EXPLORE.

Sign up for the Harlequin e-newsletter and download a free book from any series at **TryHarlequin.com**

CONNECT.

Join our Harlequin community to share your thoughts and connect with other romance readers! **Facebook.com/groups/HarlequinConnection**